# Noonalook

## T Reeves

ISBN: 9781658859776

i

For Seth, my own little Sundu.

At one time, Noonalook had been a great man, and had done great things, but not anymore. At one time Noonalook had been part of his tribe, and had a family, but not anymore. These days were his sad days, and he felt as if he couldn't bear them any longer.

# ONE

Western Europe. 35,000 B.C.

Goosebumps rose and fell on Noonalook's skin like waves on water from the crisp, autumn wind. He walked through the woods with a slight stoop and a limp, kicking the dead leaves away from the sticks hidden beneath. In his late fifties, Noonalook had aged significantly from a hard life. Silver streaked throughout his long, dirty hair and beard.

He uncovered a stick not much bigger around than his thumb and as long as his arm. It was the biggest stick he'd seen today and wondered how he had overlooked it since he scoured the forest multiple times a day. He bent to pick it up with his good arm, grunting as he stretched the long and jagged scars across his back. He cradled the stick with the others in his left arm, mangled many years ago by an enormous cave lion named Shokona. His right leg had also been chewed up and rendered nearly useless. Noonalook used the scars as his bitter reminder of the great cat that had given him the injuries, taken his family, and ruined his life.

He limped from the dense forest to the outer edge, where the trees grew smaller and farther apart, and the land opened to a vast plain covered in a sea of yellow grass. It was a gray afternoon, and the tall grasses performed a synchronized dance with the strong north wind. Noonalook dropped his armload of sticks and scanned across the vast plains. Misty, blue mountains sat in the distance on the horizon to the east. He had never been far from the forest and wondered what was there in those blue mountains. The wind whisking the long hair from his face, revealed a nasty scar running down the left side from the top of his head to his chin. He cupped his hands to his mouth. "Shokona!" he shouted as loud as he could. He waited and watched the tall grass, but saw nothing. "Shokona!" he shouted again. Still nothing. Every day he waited for the giant cat, but it never came. He gathered up his sticks again and turned to walk back through the forest. He would not die today.

The thick litter of leaves rustled across the forest floor as the wind picked them up and pushed them on. Noonalook shivered each time the cold wind blew across him. His back, chest, and legs were bare, but around his midsection, he wore the skins of raccoons, rabbits, and other small mammals sewn together by his own hand. These hides would not be enough against the coming winter, and most of them were worn thin. He had not hunted or killed the animals of the skins he wore, but found them already dead, or sneaked a hide or two from the others in the tribe. He still had the thick skins from the large animals he'd hunted and killed when he'd been younger. Around his waist was a leather belt holding a flint rock knife and across his shoulder lay a leather strap keeping a bag at his hip. He'd made the bag himself from animal skins and used it to hold things he picked up while searching for firewood. The pack currently held a few pecans he'd found on the ground.

He stopped at a lichen-covered rock and dropped the sticks next to it. He strained his mutilated muscles against the heavy stone to roll it over, and beneath it, he found a fat, white grub worm. He picked it up with dirty fingers, feeling the prickly, little legs of the worm's upper body, then put it in his mouth and swallowed it whole. Having bitten into one before, he recalled the bitterness of the juice inside the worm. This was not the kind of food he liked to eat, but for the past several years, it had been all he could catch. Nothing else hid under the stone and let it fall back into place. He picked up his sticks again and limped back to his home.

His home was located in the forest away from the village of his tribe. The tribe did not want Noonalook near them and saw the old man as a burden, but they did allow him to stay on the outskirts of their village, and he was thankful for at least that. Even though they mocked and laughed at him, any human contact was better than none. He was glad he could at least hear them talking and singing. He didn't think he could bear the loneliness if he were completely alone.

The day grew late as he neared his home. His small shelter, made from saplings, branches, grass, and animal skins, was constructed better than the other structures in the village. It was sturdy and lashed well together with the most durable cords he had braided himself. The little hut had withstood storms for years and kept him dry in the rain and reasonably warm in the winter. Even though the shelter stood only a few feet high, it was tall enough for him to sit up inside and long enough for him to stretch out.

Noonalook knew the hunting party from the village would be returning soon if they hadn't already. He hoped their hunt had been successful so he could possibly get some of their kills, even though they'd stopped sharing with him many years before. Other than an occasional snake or frog or turtle, it had been a long time since he had eaten meat. Sometimes at night, when the images came to his sleep, he saw himself eating meat and could taste it, but in the morning, he woke hungry and disappointed. He didn't like it when he saw things in his sleep and longed for the nights when there were no images.

He could now see the little village in the clearing of the forest, but the men were not there yet. As he approached his shelter, he saw the fire he kept in front of his home had burned down to orange and gray coals. He looked at the measly gathering of wood in his arms and knew it wouldn't last the night. He would have to go out again before dark to scrounge up more. Unless he could find a way to cut a tree or at least some of the lower limbs, there would not be enough wood to last the winter. He knew he was too old and too maimed to cut down trees anymore and wondered if he would survive the winter.

He dropped the wood and sat down between his shelter and the fire. He dumped the pecans near a thick, flat rock he used as a table for hammering or breaking things, such as nuts or sheering the flint rocks into razor-sharp knives and spearheads. He also had a stone he used as a hammer that perfectly fit his hand.

He stirred up the coals and placed a couple of sticks on top to keep the fire alive. He would have to rest a little before going out to find more wood. His muscles were sore, and the cold made them stiff. He reached back into his shelter and pulled out one of the thick skins he slept with. He draped it over his shoulders to keep the cold wind off of his back, then he reached back inside and pulled out an animal bladder he used as a canteen. He drank about half of the water as he watched the wood on the coals smoke and a flame appear. Sometimes when he stared into the blaze, images arose in the flickering flames, kind of like the dreams he saw as he slept. Little people and animals danced around the burning wood, and sometimes, even monsters.

He broke his gaze into the fire at the sound of leaves crunching beneath small feet. He knew it was the children from the village coming to torment him again. He tied off the bladder and put it back into his shelter. The kids ran around from behind his home, laughing.

"Noonalook! Noonalook!" They sang out in taunting tones. The filthy, long-haired little beasts ran around Noonalook, throwing rocks at him and hitting him with their sticks. He held up his arms in defense as they pounded on him. Like an animal, he growled at them and tried to stand, but they pushed him over.

One rock struck him just above his left eye, cutting him open. He grabbed a stick from one of the kids and swung it at them, giving him a chance to finally stand. He took a few menacing steps toward them, holding up the limb as if to hit them, and they ran back to the village laughing.

He broke the stick over his knee and threw the two pieces into the fire. He dabbed the blood from his cut, looking at it on his fingers for a moment before wiping it on his skins. He looked back at the village in disgust and saw the children with their mothers, pointing back at him and laughing. He sat back down and shook his head. Had they really forgotten what he had once been?

The evening had come, and Noonalook pushed the leaves around, looking for more wood. When shouting erupted from the village, Noonalook knew the hunters had returned. He looked back at the children running around the men, trying to touch the small deer they'd killed. His mouth salivated, thinking about the deer, and he kicked the leaves to get his mind off of food. He found another small branch and added it to the pathetic pile he'd already gathered.

Looking up into the trees, there were many dead limbs, but he would have to wait for a strong wind to knock them down. Far above the trees, the clouds had thickened and seemed to hang low, making the night come sooner. There would be no moonlight tonight.

Noonalook walked through the darkening forest heading back for his home. Light from the massive fire of the village was nearly blinding in the darkness as he neared his shelter. He could see the deer had been skinned, and chunks of meat now cooked over the fire. Everyone in the village was happy. The women sang songs as the children danced around the flames, and the men laughed and told stories. Noonalook was too far away to make out what they said, but he wondered if any of those stories could have been about him in the old days, but those memories made him sad.

The sun had finally set, and, except for the

fires burning about the village, the forest was dark. The wind that had blown all day had settled down, and the smell of cooked deer lingered in the air. Noonalook sat before the flames, smashing open pecans.

A dog from the village wandered by with part of a cooked leg bone from the deer. Somehow the dog had sneaked this treasure away and now looked for a safe place from the other dogs to eat it. Noonalook watched the dog circle around in the leaves on the other side of his fire and lay down. In the dark, Noonalook couldn't tell if there was any meat left on it or not, but he wasn't going to let a dog have it, either way.

He picked up a stick and ambled toward the dog. The dog stopped chewing, protected the bone under its chin, and growled deeply at Noonalook. He took another step forward, and the dog snatched the bone up and its mouth and stood as if to run away. Noonalook swung the stick, hitting the dog in the head. The dog yelped and dropped the bone. Noonalook hit the dog again on its back, and it ran away in defeat back to the village.

He picked the bone up, wiping the dirt and leaves from it. He sat back down in front of his shelter near the fire and looked over the bone in the light, finding only small bits of meat still clinging to it. He closed his eyes and brought the bone up to his nose, inhaling the smoky aroma, and remembering happier times. He let the scents linger in his head for a while, then exhaled and opened his eyes. He picked off the meat and ate it and swallowed whole the gristle he found still stuck to the bone. He moved the pecans from the smashing rock and placed the bone on it. He carefully broke the bone in two with his hammer rock. He sucked out the marrow from the two pieces, then took a long, slender twig and scraped out all he could and finished by licking the stick clean.

The taste of the meat had made him hungrier, so he returned to breaking and eating the pecans. The dryness of the nuts had made him thirsty, and he pulled out his water bladder. He drank it all, then reached inside for his other bladder and found it empty. He had forgotten to refill it. He looked into the dark forest and wished he'd remembered to get water earlier. The stream was not too far away, but he didn't look forward to walking through a dark forest without even the moonlight to help him see his way. He had a hard enough time walking through it in the daylight. He considered just waiting until morning, but he knew he wouldn't sleep well if he were hungry and thirsty. There wasn't much he could to about solving his hunger problem, but he could quench his thirst. He stood and walked slowly and carefully through the woods to the stream.

Noonalook eased himself carefully between the trees and used them to steady himself as he stepped down to the bank of the stream. He carefully lay down and drank until he was full then filled the two bladders.

When he had finished, he sat up to let the water settle in his stomach. The breeze blew lightly across the water, bringing with it the scents and sounds of the forest. There was a strange smell in the air. He moved his head about, sniffing the air, then the leaves rustled across the stream, somewhere farther back in the woods. He quickly picked up the bladders and stood, looking into the dark forest, but he couldn't see anything. He closed his eyes to concentrate and listen, slowly moving his head around in the wind to catch all the sounds he could. Something walked carefully through the leaves. It sounded like a lot of feet. A lot of human feet.

He moved quickly and quietly from the stream, finding a rotting log on the ground with vines growing over it. He crouched behind the trunk and moved some of the vines about to help him blend in better, then waited and watched.

Whispers and low voices broke through the night, and the scents became stronger as the group moved closer. Noonalook peeked over the log as people emerged from the forest to stop at the creek. It was a small tribe of about thirty with a few women and even children, and most of them drank from the stream. The men, carrying spears and knives, spoke quietly to one another, but Noonalook had never heard these words. There were other tribes in the area, but none spoke the strange words these men used.

Two of the men argued over something and pointed up to the cloudy sky over the treetops. Noonalook carefully turned to see what they were pointing at to discover the smoke plume from his village drifting over the trees. He looked back at the men as they continued to argue and point. It seemed to Noonalook that one man wanted to go around the village while the other wanted to go to it. The man wanting to go to the village pushed the other man and spoke harshly to him. Noonalook now knew which man was the chief.

Koota, the man who'd been pushed, was angry and walked back to his mate, Thera, muttering something to her. Thera held onto Sundu, a small boy of five years, listened to her husband and nodded. The chief spoke something to the tribe, then motioned toward the smoke. The tribe crossed the stream, following the chief, and the women carried their small children across to keep them dry in the cold air.

Noonalook didn't move a muscle as the tribe passed by him by only a few feet. When the tribe had gotten several yards away, Noonalook stood back up and followed quietly behind them, leaving his water bladders behind. Noonalook's mind raced with what was going to happen next. The tribe had moved too quietly and aggressively to be friendly or wanting to make trades. Noonalook imagined that there would be a raid for food or tools or women. It had happened before, but not very often. If he gave a warning cry, perhaps the village would have time to defend themselves and maybe show him favor. But there was also the likelihood that the invading tribe would kill him for giving such a warning. It could be a good way to die.

"Gee-lay!" Noonalook shouted long and loud.

# TWO

Dogs from the village barked, giving their own warning cry of strangers approaching. Then there were human shouts and screams of alarm and terror. Noonalook ran back to the village, stumbling and tripping many times in the dark as he heard the cries from his tribe grow louder and more intense. It had been a long time since he had run for anything, and he stopped to catch his breath when the village was in view. The chief and the men from his tribe fought as the invaders grabbed for the girls. The girls kicked, screamed, and cried as the men from the other tribe carried them away. Noonalook had seen it before. A tribe loses their women from sickness, childbirth, raids, or war, and the tribe must survive any way they can. Sometimes other tribes would ask to trade for women, and sometimes they just stole them. Noonalook leaned wearily against the tree, breathing hard, and watched.

Hidden in the forest on the other side of the

village, Thera crouched down and held Sundu as she watched her tribe's men fight with the villagers over the girls. There were other women at their base village far to the north but not enough for the tribe to survive. There was always death during winter, and with winter quickly approaching, they couldn't afford to lose any more. They had come looking for girls and had not been very successful. They had traveled so far and had lost more men than they had gained in women.

Sundu squirmed in her arms, wanting to go to the ground. Thera could see the men had four girls, but the villagers battled to get them back. Thera watched in horror as her mate, Koota, fought face to face with a man, but another man stabbed Koota in the back with a spear. Koota fell to his knees then to his face.

Thera stood and screamed, knocking Sundu to the ground. She picked him up and pushed him to another woman nearby who already had two small children in her arms.

Thera ran through the forest and fighting men to the village where Koota lay. She shook his shoulders, but there was no response. She rolled him onto his back, and his lifeless eyes staring past her into the night sky confirmed that he was dead. She bent over him and wept loudly.

The chief of the invading tribe saw the kidnapped girls being carried into the darkness of the forest. "Cauntolano!" he shouted.

At the chief's command, the women hiding in the forest stood and ran away with their children along with the men and screaming girls. The woman watching Sundu tried to run, but Sundu wouldn't move. "Sundu!" she shouted. "Cauntolano! Samisane! Samisane!"

Sundu was too frightened to move, not knowing where his parents were or understanding what was going on. The shouts and screams in the dark had paralyzed him with fear, and he clung tightly to a small tree. The woman pulled him while still trying to hold onto her own children, but Sundu wouldn't budge.

"Samisane!"

"Hendi!" shouted Sundu, and he pointed to the village. "Garlona! Dendaya!"

"Sundu, samisane!" she pleaded desperately and pulled him again, but the boy would not let go of the tree and tried to kick her away.

Behind Sundu, she saw the men from her tribe running away with the villagers chasing them. "Cauntolano!" she screamed. If she didn't leave now, she feared she would be left behind and captured by the angry villagers. "Cauntolano!" she begged one last time.

"Hendi!" said Sundu.

"Bendalo!" she said in exasperation and ran into the forest with the rest of her tribe, leaving Sundu by himself.

Sundu watched the woman run into the darkness and disappear. He turned back to the village, looking for his mother and father, but he only saw the dark figures running toward him. He couldn't tell if they were from his tribe or not.

Thera looked up and realized she was being left behind. She gave one last look to Koota then ran after her tribe. The invading chief and a few of his men held the villagers back with their spears as the rest escaped. Thera ran through the defense line and on into the forest. When their tribe had disappeared deep into the woods with the girls, the chief and his men followed behind. The villagers yelled and chased after them.

Thera looked for her son as she ran through the forest with the others, but she couldn't find him. "Sundu?" she called out as she ran. "Sundu?" She saw children running ahead of her and caught up with them, but none were her son. Farther ahead, she saw the woman to whom she had left Sundu, struggling to carry her two children. "Sundu!" she cried out. Thera ran harder and caught up with the woman. She grabbed the woman's arm and stopped her when she saw Sundu was no longer with her.

"Sundu, baklmo?" Thera asked.

"Hendi, lo, Sundu! Hendi lo cauntolano!" the woman explained and desperately ran on.

Thera looked back into the forest from where she just came. She heard the angry villagers getting closer. She ran toward them, looking for her son. "Sundu!" she called out as she ran. "Sundu!"

One of her tribesmen grabbed her and pulled her back. "Hendi!" she shouted, and she tried to remove herself from his grasp. She pointed back to the village. "Sundu!"

"Hendi!" the said man. They could now see the village warriors getting closer. The man pulled Thera with him.

"Sundu!" she cried. "Sundu!"

The tribe's chief caught up and helped pull the distraught woman along as she cried. They ran back across the stream and into the dark forest. Thera had lost her husband and her son. She knew Sundu was as good as dead when the angry villagers discovered him. The pain and helplessness overwhelmed her, and she felt nothing else as the men pulled her away.

When the village men finally reached the stream, they stopped. They looked into the forest and tried to listen, but they could not see or hear anything. It seemed as if the tribe had disappeared entirely. They waited for movement or whispered voices, and other than the dead leaves rubbing against each other when the breeze blew, no sound came from the forest. The chief finally turned back to his men and pointed back at their village. "Mawpumo," he said dispirited and started back

One man stepped in front of the chief, blocking his way. "Candan ta nunda!" he said and pointed across the stream.

"Stellen doe candan!" said another.

The enraged men were the fathers of the girls that had been taken. The other men standing around them grew restless and muttered to one another in low and discouraging voices.

"Mawpumo!" repeated the chief, meeting each man's eye and quietened them down. "Mawpumo," he said quietly and walked back toward their village in defeat. The men looked at one another then followed their chief back one by one until only two of the fathers remained. They looked back across the stream, knowing they would die if they chased after on their own, then turned and followed the others. As the men walked back to their village, the chief suddenly stopped and held up his hand. The others stopped and listened. Somewhere before them in the dark, they heard the sound of a child's muffled crying.

Noonalook had watched the fighting from the forest. It had happened so fast, and now it was over. He was angry with himself that he didn't get a chance to join the fight, to remind the tribe of who he had once been, and to have the opportunity to die in battle for something noble. Or to have any chance to die. He rubbed his face with both hands, then hobbled back to the village.

Seven bodies lay on the ground. Four of them were from the village, and three were from the invaders. The mates and children of the fallen men wept over the bodies of their loved ones. Noonalook stood at the edge of the village and watched for a moment, then ambled to the dead. He expected someone to chase him away or hit him with a stick or a rock, but all were still and quiet. Perhaps they still had some memory of who he was and knew he was there to help. He knelt over each of the bodies, checking for signs of life, but found none.

As he examined the last corpse, the angry men returned from the forest, shouting and pumping their fists into the air. Two men dragged a boy back into the village with them. Noonalook was only vaguely familiar with the children of the village, and this one was unknown. Had the invading tribe accidentally left behind one of their own? It seemed impossible, yet here was a strange boy. The boy was young, perhaps four, five or six, and he wore what looked like a single skin with a hole cut in the middle for his head and draped down his front and his back like a poncho and tied around the middle with cord.

Noonalook watched the boy squirm and wriggle like a wild animal in their grasp. Noonalook had been so entranced by the captured boy that he did not see the chief approach him as he still knelt over one of the bodies. The chief kicked Noonalook in the ribs hard enough to knock him over.

"Bardoni!" the chief spat out.

Noonalook crawled a safe distance away and painfully stood back to his feet while holding his ribs.

"Akinik!" the boy cried out as he tried to break free. "Akinik!" Then he saw his dead father on the ground. "Garlona! Garlona!" he screamed. He scuffled with the men to get loose and finally bit their hands to free himself. He ran to the body of his father and shook it, trying to wake him. "Garlona, clenemo! Cauntolano! Cauntolano!" he pleaded, but Koota did not move. The boy pulled on his father's arm. "Samisane!" He pulled the body with all his might and gained only a few inches.

The villagers laughed at the boy, but Noonalook did not. The village chief stepped forward with his flint knife and grabbed the boy by the hair, pulling his head back to expose his neck. "Dano den golkon sampawa!" said the chief as he put the knife to the boy's throat.

"Bongala," shouted Noonalook. It was the first time he had spoken to the villagers in a very long time, and it stopped the chief, who was just as surprised as everyone else. "Bongala!" Noonalook repeated. He beat his chest and pointed to the boy. "Kando mawn linbune," Noonalook told them. Anger and authority sounded in his voice.

The chief and the villagers stood motionless in complete silence. They looked at one another for a moment, then laughed at Noonalook as if he had been playing a joke on them. The chief smiled and looked back down at the boy to cut his throat, but before he could carry it through, the handle of a spear struck him on the head hard enough to cut open his scalp and bleed. The chief looked up in time to see Noonalook spin the spear around and jab the sharp point against the chief's throat. The laughter stopped, and Noonalook pushed the spear deeper against the chief's throat, cutting into the flesh. The leader dared not move.

"Bongala!" Noonalook said with a snarl through clenched teeth. The chief dropped the knife and released the boy. Sundu turned and looked up at the man who nearly killed him, seeing the blood from the top of his head and neck, then turned back to look at the scarred old man with the spear. Noonalook pointed to Sundu and motioned for him to come.

"Tooga," Noonalook said gently. He held out the hand with the mangled arm to Sundu. "Tooga," he said once more. Sundu wiped his eyes and looked around at those who wanted to kill him then ran to Noonalook. Noonalook pulled the spear away from the chief's throat and threw it aside. Noonalook took the boy's hand and looked at the villagers with the sternness they had not seen in years. Noonalook gently pulled the boy toward his shelter. The villagers watched them walk away, then looked back at the chief. The chief wiped the blood from his head and looked at his red hand.

"Spendan uku!" he said to Noonalook, but the old one did not bother to stop or even look back. The chief looked back at his people, who stood silent and motionless. He pointed to the bodies and motioned for the mess to be swept away, then stomped into his shelter.

Noonalook led the crying boy to his shelter and made him sit in front of the fire. The boy was scared, and Noonalook knew he would have to get the boy back to his own tribe, and if he could hurry, maybe he could find them. This village didn't need another outcast.

Noonalook crawled inside his shelter and grabbed up his own spear and knife. When he came back out, the boy was not there and found him running through the forest. Noonalook chased after him. It was terrible enough for Noonalook to run with his mangled leg, but running through the dark forest was incredibly tricky. He tripped and fell many times, but he was still able to keep track of the boy ahead of him. Before long, Noonalook caught up with Sundu and grabbed him by the arm. "Bongala!" he told Sundu.

Sundu wriggled in his grasp to get free. "Hendi," Sundu shouted. "Hendi!"

He bit Noonalook's hand hard enough to draw blood, and Noonalook let him go. Sundu ran again, but Noonalook swept the handle of his spear at the boy's feet, tripping him, then swung it again, striking the boy on the back. Sundu cried out in pain. Noonalook stepped on the boys back and pinned him to the ground, then he looked out into the darkness toward the stream but could not see or hear anyone.

"Shundolla," shouted Noonalook in the direction the tribe had run. He heard no reply. "Shundolla!" he repeated. He waited a moment for a response, then removed his foot from the boy's back and helped him up. Surely someone was missing this boy. Wouldn't they try to rescue him? Noonalook dragged Sundu by the arm farther into the forest. They arrived at the stream, and he could not see anyone there. "Shundolla," he shouted across the creek.

Sundu watched Noonalook as he yelled the unfamiliar word across the water. Noonalook looked down at the sniffling boy and motioned for Sundu to shout by opening his fingers and mouth at the same time, as if his fingers were words. Then he took the boy's face and squeezed his cheeks in and out and moved his jaw up and down, trying to make him talk.

"Shundolla!" Noonalook said as he pressed the boy's cheeks together again.

Sundu seemed to catch on finally and brought his free hand up to his mouth. "Gartu!" he shouted. He looked up at Noonalook. Noonalook smiled, showing his broken, brown teeth and nodded his head in approval. It suddenly dawned on Noonalook that he couldn't remember the last time he had smiled, and it felt different to his face. He squeezed Sundu's cheeks together once more. "Gartu," Sundu shouted again.

"Gartu," Noonalook shouted. He didn't know the significance of the word, but it meant something to the boy, and that implied that it meant something to the tribe. Perhaps the tribe's own language from the boy would get their attention. He'd been holding the boy with his maimed arm, and it had become painful. Noonalook released him, and Sundu ran again. Noonalook grabbed him with his good hand and picked him up. Sundu hit and kicked Noonalook fiercely as he was carried across the cold stream. Noonalook set him down on the other side but still kept a firm grip on him. "Gartu," he shouted again and pulled Sundu farther into the forest.

Deep in the forest, Thera and the leader of the tribe heard Noonalook's voice shouting "gartu." Thera looked at the chief and tried to run back, but he held onto her.

"Hendi," he whispered quietly to her. "Dono tu gaunan." The chief pantomimed being stabbed with a knife in his chest, fearing it was a trap in retaliation of their raid. There would be no other reason to call them back. He knew Sundu had gotten lost, and the village, more than likely, was using the boy as bait for a counterattack. He knew they could not rescue the boy. More of their people could die if they tried, and they had already lost so many lives in the past few months. They could not afford any more losses. The chief put his arm around the crying mother and pulled her along, wishing there could be another way.

After walking briskly several yards through the woods, Noonalook and Sundu stopped. Noonalook listened intensely to the forest, hoping to pick out any sound made by the boy's tribe should they be close by. Still, he heard nothing except the night birds, crickets, and a few frogs. "Gartu," he shouted as loud as he could. He waited and listened for an answer to his call, but none came. How could they leave the boy behind? Somebody has to know he was not with them. Someone has to miss him.

He looked down at Sundu and remembered

how he had reacted to the dead man. Had that been his father? It had to be someone close to him, or he would not have carried on that way. Is the reason no one had missed him because his mother was dead, too? Either way, the boy belonged with his tribe. He would die if he stayed here. Noonalook looked back into the forest. "Shundolla!" he then cried out.

He hadn't used his voice very much lately, and his throat hurt from the yelling. He and Sundu stood still and listened for a while longer until he felt the boy shivering in his hand from the cold night air. "Kendowen," he said, looking down at Sundu. Sundu tried to squirm away, but Noonalook kept a firm grip on him. He dropped painfully down to one knee and met the small boy's eyes. Sundu stopped moving. This boy reminded him of his own son when he had been that age, and those painful memories he tried to keep buried deep inside rose to the surface. His own son had been not much older than this boy when he had died. "Kendowen," he said again. He closed his eyes and pretended to sleep then wake. "Kendowen." He repeated the pretend sleeping and waking. He wished the boy understood that he was trying to help him. He knew the boy was scared, but he didn't know what else to do for him. They both needed sleep, and they could take off in the morning to catch up with the tribe. He slowly stood back up and walked back to the village with Sundu.

"Hendi," Sundu shouted and pulled against Noonalook.

Noonalook picked him up again and put him over his shoulder like a sack and carried him back across the stream with Sundu kicking and hitting him.

Noonalook stopped at the log where he'd left

the water bladders earlier. He put Sundu down, then picked up the water bladders and handed them to Sundu to carry. Giving Noonalook an angry look, Sundu dropped them to the ground. Noonalook swatted the back of the boy's legs with his spear handle then pointed at the bladders. Sundu stared at Noonalook with hatred in his eyes, then reluctantly picked up the two water containers.

Noonalook guided him back to the village with Sundu crying the whole time. A few of the village men restlessly paced the village perimeter with their spears, cautious of another attack. They stopped to watch the old man escort the boy back to his shelter. The village women peeked from their huts after they heard the boy crying.

Noonalook took the bladders from Sundu and forced him to sit next to the dying fire. When Noonalook put the bladders back in his shelter, the boy got up and ran again. Noonalook chased after and tackled him. The villagers laughed at Noonalook and his new problem as Noonalook dragged Sundu back and pushed him back down in front of the fire. He held onto Sundu with his deformed hand while he reached into his shelter and pulled out some braided cord. He tied Sundu's hands behind him and then tied his feet. Sundu rolled and bucked and cried the entire time.

When Noonalook had finished, he sat the boy back up by the fire. Dirt and bits of leaves had mixed with the mucus from Sundu's runny nose and had smeared across his face. Noonalook wiped the snotty mud from the boy with his hand, then rubbed it on his own skins. He pulled out one of the thick furs and put it over Sundu's shoulders to warm him. Defeated,

Sundu put his head down and wept quietly. Noonalook put his spear and knife back in the shelter and crawled inside. He laid out more furs on one side for Sundu to sleep on. Once he got it ready, he reached out and pulled the boy inside. Sundu screamed and thrashed about, reminding Noonalook of a fish out of water.

Noonalook rolled Sundu to one side of the shelter and covered him with the skins, but he still squirmed about. Noonalook pushed Sundu gently and kept him there until he calmed down. Noonalook pushed all of his belongings against the door, then tied a cord around his foot and the other to Sundu's foot, in case he tried to escape during the night. Noonalook then crawled to the other side of the shelter and lay down. He was tired and hadn't had that much action in a long time. He sighed, then covered himself with one of the thick skins, listening to the boy cry. Before long, the crying stopped, and Sundu was quiet, then Noonalook finally fell asleep.

# THREE

Noonalook woke before dawn, breathing heavily and wet with sweat from the dream. He lay under his warm skins, feeling the cold on his face, and thought about the things he had seen when he slept. The spirits that had visited him in the night had disturbed him, and their presence still lingered like the taste of a bitter nut stuck to your tongue. He'd had the dreams for many years and hated the way they made him feel.

He rolled over when he heard Sundu breathing and saw him sleeping beneath the pile of skins. Having gotten used to living alone for so long, he'd forgotten about the boy. Noonalook was reminded again of his own son, and he sat up to rub his eyes, breaking the yellow crust from them and yawned. Sometimes the memories were just as bad as the nightmares. He quietly untied himself from Sundu, picked up his knife and his shoulder bag and crawled outside.

It was still dark, but the eastern part of the sky was faintly growing brighter. The clouds had thinned out, letting a few stars peek through and below on the ground, little clouds of mist spotting the forest floor glowed a ghostly white. A lone bird had woken early and chirped somewhere in the forest. Noonalook squatted beside the fire and stirred up the coals, trying to get the dreams out of his head. He tossed the remaining sticks on the coals, then stood and walked into the forest.

He came to the stream, which also had little clouds floating over it. In the increasing light, the footprints of the tribe from the night before were still visible in the mud. The boy's tribe had a good head start, but Noonalook was sure he could catch up to them and give them back their boy. He knew that once the tribe had gotten far enough away, they would slow down, and that's where Noonalook would catch them.

He knelt down and drank from the stream, then splashed water in his face and over his head. This was the best way he had found to evict the spirits from his head. The water was cold, but it felt good, and it tasted good. He stood and stretched, reminding himself he had to find food for himself and for the boy. It had been a long time since he had to care for anyone else.

Noonalook returned home with more sticks, and his shoulder bag full. He stirred up the coals and placed some of the sticks he'd gathered over them. He looked inside the shelter where Sundu still slept. He pulled out one of the skins he had slept with and wrapped it around himself as he scooted closer to the fire.

He emptied the contents of the bag on his smashing rock and looked over the treasures he had gathered. He had found some walnuts, more pecans, an egg, some minnows, and a small frog he had killed. He cut open the frog's belly with his knife, pulled out the insides, then dropped them into his mouth and swallowed them whole. He took a small, straight branch and pushed it into the frog's mouth and out its backside. He fashioned the stick to where the frog hovered over the flames. He took the egg and set it next to the fire where it could cook slowly but not burn. He cracked the walnuts and the pecans and picked out and ate the meat from them. He carefully rotated the frog and the egg.

Noonalook had made enough noise cracking the nuts that he had woken Sundu. Noonalook could hear the boy thrashing about inside the shelter, trying to break free of his bonds. The old man reached inside and grabbed the boy's leg, but released it when he felt moisture. He looked at his wet hand and smelled it. The boy had peed on himself. He reached back into the shelter, and angrily pulled the boy outside.

"Kono paum toogeen?" Noonalook asked in a hot temper. He could tell the boy did not understand what he was saying. He pointed to the soaking skin the boy wore. "Kono paum toogeen?" he asked again.

Sundu seemed to understand what the old man was yelling about and wriggled around to show Noonalook his hands and feet were tied. Noonalook hadn't thought about the boy needing to go pee in the night. Sundu glared at Noonalook. Noonalook smiled apologetically and helped the boy sit up and scooted him closer to the fire.

Picking up the cooking frog, Noonalook

examined the meat and smelled it. He took a small bite, then held the rest up to Sundu's mouth. Sundu wrinkled his nose and turned his face away. Noonalook moved the frog again to the boy's mouth, but Sundu turned his face again, avoiding the frog.

Noonalook was puzzled. Surely the boy must be hungry, yet he acted otherwise. Maybe the boy didn't understand. "Stemma," he said as he pulled a piece of meat from the frog and pushed it into the boy's mouth.

Sundu immediately spat it to the ground. Noonalook looked at the boy then down at the meat. He picked it up and put it back into Sundu's mouth, but he only spat it out again. Noonalook took a stick and swatted at the boy's leg with it, then picked up the meat and held it before Sundu once more. The boy turned his head away.

"Uhh," said Noonalook, and he put the piece of meat into his own mouth.

He offered the rest of the frog to Sundu, but he again declined, so Noonalook ate the rest of the frog. He then pulled the egg away from the fire and put it in the grass to cool. He didn't know what kind of egg it was, but he had found it near the stream. It was always a rare and pleasant treat to find an egg. Noonalook picked up some of the crushed nuts and carefully picked out the meat. He offered a small handful to Sundu, who once again refused, so Noonalook ate them also.

The egg had cooled enough to handle now. Sundu watched out of the corner of his eye as the old man carefully broke open the top of the shell. The egg was only partially cooked and still runny inside. Noonalook sniffed it then looked at the boy. The egg smelled delicious, and Noonalook would have loved to have eaten it also, but he had a different plan for the egg. He put the egg under Sundu's nose, and he rejected it. Noonalook took a small stick and stirred the egg then licked it off. He grabbed Sundu's hair, pulled his head back, and poured the egg down the boy's throat. Noonalook covered Sundu's mouth with his hand until the boy had swallowed the egg. Noonalook removed his hand as Sundu choked and coughed. He was glad the boy had eaten now. Enraged, Sundu attempted to throw a tantrum but had a difficult time being tied up, so he gave up the idea and just lay on the ground and cried.

Noonalook crawled back into his shelter, where he rolled up his thick skins and tied them with straps. He then tied a long rope around them so he could carry them on his back. He packed up his flint for making fire and extra spearheads, along with the two bladders of water in his shoulder bag. Noonalook packed everything he could carry. He didn't want the tribe thinking he was leaving forever and rob him of everything. He guessed he might be gone a week or so at the most, but he had learned that it was better to bring something and not need it than to need it and not have it.

He crawled back out of the shelter to find Sundu squirming on the ground like a worm trying to escape again. Noonalook put the skins and bag down and pulled Sundu back to the fire. He sat the boy up and knelt in front of him. He took Sundu's face in his hand and pointed with the other out into the forest.

"Jeeninum," he said to the boy. He patted Sundu on the chest, then tapped his own chest and pointed to the forest again. "Jeeninum nonuntu." The boy didn't understand. Noonalook tried to make a sign with his hands, indicating a woman's breasts. "Jeeninum," Noonalook said. "Jeeninum." He pantomimed again.

"Jeeninum?" asked Sundu.

Noonalook smiled and nodded his head. "Jeeninum nonuntu," he repeated. This time he pointed to his eyes then pointed his fingers out as if looking. "Nonuntu. Nonuntu.'

"Jeeninum?" asked Sundu again.

Noonalook pantomimed the female breasts again and nodded. "Jeeninum."

"Dendaya," said Sundu.

Noonalook hadn't heard that word before. "Den...denda?"

"Dendaya," said Sundu.

"Dendaya," repeated Noonalook. He pantomimed breasts again. "Dendaya?" Sundu smiled this time and nodded. Noonalook then patted his own chest and said, "Noonalook. Noonalook." He patted Sundu's chest. "Uh?" But Sundu only looked at him. Noonalook patted the boy's chest once more. "Uh?" He patted his own chest again. "Noonalook."

"Noonalook," said Sundu.

Noonalook smiled and nodded. "Noonalook," he said, patting his chest. He patted Sundu again. "Uh?"

"Sundu," said the boy.

"Sundu," Noonalook repeated. "Sundu."

Sundu nodded his head. "Sundu," he said, smiling.

Noonalook touched Sundu's chest, then his own chest, and pointed out to the forest. "Sundu,

Noonalook dendaya nonuntu," he said, then held up the tied skins and his bag packed full for Sundu to see and pointed again into the forest. Did the boy finally understand? Noonalook wasn't sure, but at least they knew each other's names now.

He put his things down, then knelt down and untied Sundu's feet. If the boy ran away when he was free, then he had not understood Noonalook's message. Noonalook turned Sundu around, and untied the boy's hands and put the ropes into his bag.

Noonalook stood as Sundu rubbed the red indentions on his wrists and ankles where he'd been tied. Noonalook offered his hand to Sundu and helped him stand, then he picked up his traveling supplies and his spear. He felt a relief that the boy had not run away and was confident that their journey would be better if the boy understood he was only trying to help him.

Noonalook adjusted the skins on his back, and the bag over his shoulder then looked back at the village. The villagers prepared for the burial of their men killed last night. The bodies had been separated into villagers and invaders. The female mates of those killed cooked the final meal for their husbands. The wise man knelt over the bodies of his friends and spoke magic words, which only he was allowed to speak. He painted specific markings on their faces to bless their hunts in the next life. Beyond the village, men dug holes for the dead.

He didn't want to stay and watch the ritual because he had experienced it many times before. He knew that once the holes had been dug, the bodies would be placed inside, along with their knives, spears, and extra skins to keep them warm. Their wives would put the food in with them to take on their journey to the other side. The wise man would say more magic words, then finally, the men would cover the bodies with soil.

For the first time since the men had been killed, Noonalook felt sad. Even though no one in the village no longer cared for him, Noonalook had once been part of their tribe, and he had known those men since they had been born. He had helped teach many of them how to hunt, fish, and fight. He knew they were good men, and he would miss them.

He looked down at Sundu, who was also watching the village. Noonalook knew he must be wondering what would happen to the men from his tribe. He was glad they did not share the same language because he did not want to tell him the awful truth. If the dead were an enemy, the bodies would be dragged deep into the forest and offered to Shokona, the great cat, or to Mundul, the wolf. There would be no final meal for them. Nor would there be magic words spoken over them or sacred markings painted on them. They would have no help from the village on their journey to the afterlife.

Noonalook took Sundu by the arm and led him away from the village and into the forest. He stopped to look at his home once more. He didn't know when he would return or if he would even be able to make it back. He didn't know if the other tribe would kill him or if he would get lost. He shook his head to make the discouraging thoughts go away, and they continued on into the forest.

They stopped at the stream where they could still see the footprints of Sundu's tribe. Noonalook pointed down at the prints for Sundu to see.

"Dendaya," he said, and the boy smiled. Noonalook bent down to drink and motioned for Sundu to do the same. Sundu did not refuse.

They drank until they felt they could drink no more. Noonalook didn't know when they might be able to find water again, and the two water bladders would not last them very long.

They crossed the stream and followed the trail of the tribe through the upset fallen leaves on the forest floor. It was an easy trail to follow. A rabbit ran across their path far ahead of them and hid. The rabbit reminded Noonalook that he and the boy would need food, and it concerned him. He had not hunted or even been able to hunt for a long time. If he could barely provide food for himself, how was he to provide food for both of them?

# FOUR

Noonalook and Sundu followed the trail through the forest for hours. They found some blackberry bushes with berries still on them, and picked the bushes clean, eating some and saving some. They had also run across many nut trees and gathered all they could find, putting them in Noonalook's shoulder bag. Noonalook was glad the boy was finally eating now. He supposed Sundu finally understood now that he was trying to help and take him back to his tribe and whoever there missed him.

After walking for a while, Noonalook glanced back and noticed Sundu wasn't with him. His heart skipped a beat, and his eyes darted back through the forest behind him. Had the boy run away again? He hadn't acted as if he would earlier.

He started backtracking his steps. Had something happened to him or had something snatched him? It couldn't have been any of his tribe. They would never have followed him this far out, and besides, they were burying their dead. Had an animal taken him? Shokona? Surely he would have heard something if that had occurred. "Sundu?" he called out. He listened but heard nothing. "Sundu?"

"Ay," the boy said, but Noonalook couldn't see him.

"Sundu?" he asked again and saw movement behind a bush. Then he saw the top of the boys head. Noonalook ran to him with his spear, ready to defend the boy against whatever was behind that bush. He ran around the bush then stopped and lowered the spear when he saw Sundu crouched down behind it, looking at a small box turtle. Noonalook relaxed and motioned for Sundu to come. Sundu picked up the turtle and followed Noonalook. Noonalook tried to get him to put the turtle in his bag, but the boy wanted to carry it, and Noonalook didn't argue.

They continued through the forest when something behind them moved through the thicket, and they stopped. Noonalook looked back but didn't see anything. Whatever had made the noise sounded large and heavy. It wasn't a squirrel or rabbit, but more like a man or larger.

"Shundolla?" Noonalook called out. His eyes scanned about, looking for something out of place. "Shundolla?" he asked louder. There was no reply or any other movement. He looked down at Sundu, who was more interested in the turtle than whatever had made the noise, and he motioned to go. "Tooga," he said, and they proceeded on through the forest.

After another hour or so, the forest began to thin out, and they entered an immense plain with high yellow grasses billowing in the west wind. Faint mountains lay on the horizon to the west and north. Across the golden plains, patches of trees scattered about here and there as far as the eye could see. Noonalook had not been on this side of the forest since he had been a hunter many years ago. The trail cut through the tall grass and led to the north. Noonalook knelt to study the path. There were too many broken and trampled grasses to be an animal unless it could've been a herd, but herds didn't travel in a single file. There were also no grasses cut short from grazing and no hoof prints or dung. This was a trail created by human feet.

Noonalook stood with the help of his spear and followed the path with his eyes. The tribe had walked single file through the grass, trying to hide their trail. He looked back at Sundu, sitting in the grass and playing with the turtle. Noonalook pointed at the path then up to the distant mountains where it seemed to lead. One peak stood out and reminded Noonalook of a crow's head. "Dendaya," said Noonalook.

"Dendaya?" asked Sundu in an excited tone. He stood and looked at the trail, then around, as if expecting to see his mother.

"Junja, junja," said Noonalook, pointing up and over the plains at the mountains. "Dendaya junja."

"Dendaya junja," repeated Sundu with an unclear look on his face.

Noonalook smiled and walked down the trail. "Tooga." Sundu followed, carrying his turtle.

The day had gotten late, and Noonalook and Sundu had eaten all of the berries and nuts they had picked earlier. Sundu still carried the turtle, but Noonalook knew it wouldn't be enough for the two of them to eat. There were barely any trees out on the plains, and for one to be a fruit or a nut-producing tree would be a miracle, but there were rabbits in the tall grasses. He had seen the evidence of them by the grasses moving and bending as the rabbits ran through them.

Noonalook worried about the food. How could he hunt? Even if his body was restored to the way it used to be, he didn't have the magic hunting marks on his face, nor did he have the magic words said over him. He hoped some spirit would be kind to them when it was realized that he and the boy would starve with nothing to eat. He knew the food wouldn't be dropped in his lap. He would have to find it, and if the spirit was sympathetic, it would help them. There was food all around, hopping and playing in the grasses nearby, but could he really kill a rabbit? He still knew how to hunt. He had done it for so long it had become part of his nature, but his body wouldn't work the way it was supposed to. Perhaps he could at least try.

He stopped and unloaded everything except for his spear. After leaving his belongings on the trail so he wouldn't lose it in the tall grass, he walked back to Sundu, who watched him with a curious expression. Noonalook put his hands on the boy's shoulders.

"Naungaw," Noonalook said and pointed at the ground. Already he saw that Sundu did not understand. This time Noonalook put his palm flat against the boy's chest. "Naungaw," he said again and pointed at the ground. Sundu looked down but didn't see anything. Noonalook stepped away from Sundu, thinking the boy would stay put, then turned and walked into the wind.

"Dendaya," Sundu said, pointing down the trail.

Noonalook looked back. "Naungaw," he said, holding up his hand.

He turned back to the wind and ambled on, looking for movement in the grass. Sundu watched Noonalook for a bit but grew bored. He picked up Noonalook's things left on the trail and draped them over his shoulders then continued by himself.

Noonalook saw Sundu leaving. "Sundu, naungaw!" Noonalook said, trying not to be too loud, but at the same time, emphasize that he wanted the boy to stay where he was. Sundu looked back at the old man. Noonalook moved the spear in a stabbing motion at the ground, then held up his fist with two fingers sticking up, attempting to represent a rabbit, and bounced his hand about in the air.

Sundu pointed back down the trail. "Dendaya."

"Naungaw," Noonalook said once more and motioned for the boy to stop. "Stemma," he said, then pantomimed eating, but Sundu pointed to the trail again. Frustrated, Noonalook turned back to the tall grass to search for rabbits. All of this talking would frighten the rabbits away. He let the boy walk on by himself, knowing he wouldn't get very far. He moved slowly so as not to cause any vibrations or sounds through the waist-high grass.

"Dendaya!" Sundu shouted behind Noonalook.

Noonalook had to ignore him. If there were any rabbits out here, he would miss their movement if he kept turning back to Sundu. He concentrated on the grass and recalled the hunting skills he had used long ago.

As the wind blew the grass about, he looked for subtle movements in the grass not caused by the wind. He continued in this slow manner until he saw a patch of grass moving opposite of the blowing wind. Noonalook froze as the grass bent and parted one way and then another in front of him. He watched the direction of the movement and stepped carefully in the same direction to meet whatever was moving about in the grass. He was sure the thing in the grass was a rabbit; the movements were too quick to be a possum or some other slower mammal. When the animal stopped, Noonalook stopped, and when the animal moved, he moved, masking the sound he made with the sound the animal made. He raised his spear, and his muscles tensed. His breathing slowed, and he focused on the spot of grass to the point of seeing and hearing nothing else. The animal moved, then he moved, drawing closer together in a sort of bizarre dance.

When he had gotten a spear's length from the animal, he made a screech like an eagle. The animal froze into place, and the grass stopped moving. Noonalook pinpointed precisely where the animal was. He thrust his spear forward and hit something. A rabbit jumped up, slinging blood across the flaxen grasses and ran. Noonalook chased after the rabbit. He knew the rabbit had been severely wounded and would not make it much farther or longer.

He followed the twisting and turning blood trail through the grass. He soon found the rabbit lying on its side, panting with a look of terror in its black eyes as it slowly died. Noonalook had done it, and he smiled. He wished his tribe could have seen this. He had done it without magic or ritual, and if he did have help, it was from some merciful spirit who had felt sympathy for him and the boy.

Noonalook picked up the rabbit by the hind legs, and it struggled weakly to get free. "Sundu!" Noonalook shouted, and he raised the rabbit over his head with the blood running down his arm.

Sundu stopped and looked back. His look of anger changed to joy when he saw the rabbit. He smiled and ran back to Noonalook. Noonalook hurried back through the grass to met Sundu. He dropped the dead rabbit in front of the boy.

"Stemma!" shouted Noonalook with his arms high in the air and a smile on his face as he danced a short, crippled dance in front of the rabbit and Sundu.

Sundu took a step back, frightened of Noonalook's sudden and uncharacteristic enthusiasm. Noonalook realized he'd scared the boy and patted him kindly on the head, then took his belongings from Sundu and returned them across his shoulder. Sundu squatted down and stroked the rabbit's soft, bloody fur. Noonalook picked up the rabbit, and Sundu stood, wiping his hands on his skins.

"Stemma," said Noonalook, indicating the rabbit.

"Stemma?" asked Sundu.

Noonalook pretended to eat the rabbit. "Stemma," he said again.

Sundu pointed to the trail then off to the mountains where the path led. "Dendaya?" he asked.

Noonalook smiled and nodded his head. "Dendaya." Then he started down the trail again with

Sundu following and still carrying his turtle.

They traveled on the trail the rest of the day, and when it began to grow dark, Noonalook looked for a place to stay the night. There were patches of small trees and scrub bushes across the prairie, but none were close to the trail, and he didn't want to be too far from the path. Noonalook had been watching for signs of where the tribe had stayed for the night. He knew they had small children with them, and they would have to stop somewhere to rest and sleep, but he had found no evidence of it. The trail turned from a single file to spread out, and, more than once, Noonalook and Sundu had to avoid stepping in human excrement. There appeared to be no attempt to hide their trail now, and the tribe must have assumed they were not being followed any longer.

About a mile ahead, Noonalook saw a group of trees and thought it would be the best place to stay the night. He was hungry, and he knew the boy was, too. The rabbit had stiffened in his hand, and no longer dripped blood. Their water supply was close to empty, and he would have to find water soon.

The trail eventually led near the trees Noonalook had spotted earlier. Arriving at the tree cluster, he dropped the rabbit and his belongings, then gathered wood for the fire. When Sundu saw what Noonalook was doing, he placed the turtle upside down and put a heavy stone on its belly to keep it from running away. He then joined Noonalook to search for firewood, and they wandered around the little grove of trees, finding plenty of wood.

Noonalook dropped his armload of wood

near the rabbit and began sorting the sticks to build a fire. Sundu dropped the sticks he had found near Noonalook's pile then hurried off to get more. Noonalook dug in his pack and pulled out a small pouch. He ground up some dried grass then stood small sticks into the shape of a teepee over the crushed grass. He dropped two flint rocks into his hand from his pouch then leaned in close to the sticks. He struck one stone across the other several times, making sparks. He tried to aim the sparks at the pulverized grass and continued hitting the rocks together.

Minutes later, one of the sparks hit directly in the grass at just the right spot, and a slight wisp of smoke arose. Noonalook dropped the stones and picked up the smoldering grass. He brought the wad close to his lips and gently blew into it. The smoke swelled thicker, and a smile came to his lips. He blew a little harder, and a flame appeared.

He set the burning grass back into the pyramid of sticks and added more grass and tiny twigs. He lay on his stomach, putting his face near the flames, and blew until he felt the heat on his face and smelled the singeing of his hair. He pushed himself up and added longer sticks to the fire.

Before long, the fire blazed, and its warmth felt good. Sundu returned with another armload of sticks and dropped them into the pile. He sat down with a long stick and poked at the fire. Noonalook picked up the rabbit and stood. "Sundu," he called.

Sundu looked up to see Noonalook standing over him with the dead rabbit and a long stick in one hand and a flint knife in the other, and he motioned for Sundu to follow. They walked a few feet from the fire and sat back down. Sundu sat across from Noonalook with the rabbit between them.

Sundu watched as Noonalook used the knife to cut a ring around the rabbit's neck and rings around its legs. He then turned the rabbit onto its back and cut from its neck down its tail. He carefully removed the skin as if he were taking off a suit of clothes from the rabbit. The pungent odor of the rabbit's insides drifted through the air.

Noonalook pulled out the entrails in one big handful from the carcass and placed them on the rabbit's hide, separating the heart, kidneys, and liver from the rest of the guts. He then took the long stick and sharpened one end with the knife to a point. He jabbed the long stick down the rabbit's throat and out through its backside, as he had done with the frog, placing the rabbit in the middle of the stick.

Noonalook observed Sundu watching what he was doing. Noonalook didn't know if Sundu had ever been shown how to skin, prepare, and cook a rabbit or not, but he seemed interested in what he was doing. He hadn't taught anyone in a long time, and it felt good to pass on some of his knowledge.

The rabbit cooked over the flames held up by two forked sticks on either side of the fire. Skewered over the flames also roasted the heart, liver, and kidneys. Sundu played and explored under the trees nearby while Noonalook sat next to the fire and scraped the fleshy side of the rabbit's skin with his knife. Once he had all of the flesh and fat scraped away, he pushed two more sticks into the ground a few inches apart near the fire. He draped the skin over with the fleshy side facing the flames to cure.

Even though the rabbit skin was small, it could be sewn together with other furs.

Noonalook removed the small organs from the fire. It didn't take long for them to cook. He waved them about on the stick to cool, then ate them as he watched Sundu play. Noonalook checked on the roasting rabbit, turning it occasionally. When the rabbit finished cooking, he pulled it from the fire and set it in the grass to cool.

"Sundu, stemma!" Noonalook called.

Sundu came running back with another turtle, which he showed off proudly, and Noonalook laughed. Sundu set the new turtle upside down next to the other turtle and placed a rock on its belly also.

It wasn't long before the only thing left of the rabbit was the empty, broken bones. Sundu jumped up to play again while Noonalook lay on his back. It was the first time in a long time he had been satisfied with enough food to eat. For years he had gone to bed hungry and woke up hungry.

He looked up at the sky. The sun had set, and the stars shined. There were clouds on the horizon, but they were not the clouds that brought the rain. He would not have to make a shelter for the night. He had enough skins and firewood to keep them warm. He began to feel sleepy, and he sat back up. All of the walking and the full stomach were affecting him.

He unrolled the furs and laid them out for himself and Sundu with the fire between them. Noonalook sat on his hide and pulled his bag and spear close to him. Sundu came out of the woods, sat on his fur, and drank some of the water from the bladder. He watched as Noonalook pulled a cord from his bag and tied one end around his ankle and the other end to the leftover rabbit guts. He threw the guts out past his feet then lay down with his spear beside him.

Noonalook saw Sundu looking at him with curiosity across his face. Noonalook pantomimed stabbing something at his feet with the spear, and Sundu smiled. Noonalook's father had shown him this trick when he was a boy. It usually worked if there was an animal brave, dumb, or hungry enough to get close to humans and their fire.

Noonalook lay back on his skin, and Sundu imitated him. They watched the clouds drift slowly across the starry sky. After a while, Sundu sang a little song. Noonalook had never heard the song before. It was a simple song with only a few words and notes repeated, but it was a pleasant song. The child's singing brought back memories to Noonalook of his son singing similar songs. Noonalook felt strange, for he was both happy and sad at the same time.

Eventually, the song became softer and softer until he could no longer hear it. He looked over and saw Sundu sound asleep, then he looked back up at the stars and thought once again of his son who had been dead for years now. He smiled when he thought of his son, now a man in the afterlife, hunting and taking care of his mother. Noonalook fell asleep thinking how proud he was of him.

Something pulled Noonalook's leg and woke him up. He lay still and opened his eyes, not sure if he had dreamed it until he felt another tug. The fire had died down to only glowing embers, but it was enough for Noonalook to raise his head slightly and see a badger eating the rabbit guts. He felt the spear in his hand and tightened his grip on it. He did not want to go chasing the badger out in the dark, so his aim had to be true.

He slowly lifted the spear while at the same time, pulling it back. He took a deep breath and thrust the spear into the badger. The badger screamed, waking Sundu in terror. Sundu jumped to his feet, stumbling sleepily about, and raised his hands as if to fight off an attacker. The badger tried to pull itself off of the spear and chewed and scratched at it.

Noonalook stood, taking the spear in both hands and shoved the spear entirely through the animal, pinning it to the ground. After a moment, the badger stopped screaming and thrashing and finally lay quiet. Noonalook relaxed his grip on the spear and looked over at Sundu. Sundu stared at the dead badger with wide, black eyes, and his thin chest rose and sank as he breathed heavily. Noonalook sputtered out a laugh. Sundu looked at Noonalook, still terrified, then smiled and finally laughed.

"Stemma," laughed Noonalook. He pulled the spear from the badger and heaved the animal closer to their camp. He threw more wood on the fire and sat back down. He tossed the guts out beyond his feet once more and lay back down with the spear again.

"Stemma," Sundu repeated with a sigh and a smile. He lay back down, and soon they were both asleep again.

Sometime later in the night, Noonalook woke abruptly by being jerked and dragged from his bed. He cried out in confusion and fear and flailed his arms, trying to grab his spear. Sundu was once again startled awake and jumped to his feet, and what he saw terrified him.

A cave lion, standing taller than a man's waist, had the rabbit guts and rope in its mouth and dragged Noonalook on his back. Noonalook's screaming and kicking scared the cave lion into running.

"Noonalook," Sundu screamed.

It took a Noonalook a couple of seconds to clear the hazy sleep from his brain enough to realize what was happening to him. He recognized the cave lion as Shokona, the great cat, the great cat that had killed his family. In the firelight, Noonalook saw the scars dotting the animal's fur. They were the scars he had put there.

Noonalook found his knife still in his waist belt and tried to cut the cord, but he couldn't reach it; his mangled muscles didn't allow him that flexibility. He stabbed the blade into the ground, trying to stop the lion's run, but Shokona was strong, and the knife pulled from his hand.

Noonalook rolled over on his stomach and clawed the ground, grasping for anything. He looked back at Sundu chasing after him, and carrying the spear that was twice his height.

"Sundu," Noonalook cried out. He saw Sundu's little legs running as fast as they could, trying to catch up. Sundu held out the spear handle to Noonalook as he ran. He eventually got close enough for Noonalook to grab the spear. Noonalook rolled over on his back again and used the spearhead to reach down and cut through the rope. The cord snapped, and Noonalook rolled to a stop. He watched Shokona disappear into the darkness. Noonalook lay on his back for a moment, trying to catch his breath. Sundu ran to him and dropped to his knees. He was even more out of breath than Noonalook was. The boy patted Noonalook's dirty hair.

"Sondul dee lo sullden dee?" asked Sundu.

Noonalook heard the concern and fear and Sundu's voice and thought he understood the meaning. Noonalook smiled and nodded, putting his hand on Sundu's shoulder. The boy had shown bravery and had saved his life. Sundu was a very good boy, Noonalook thought.

They stood and walked back to the fire, picking up Noonalook's knife along the way. When they got to the firelight, Noonalook could see that Sundu had been crying, and he put his arm around the boy. Sundu looked up at him and smiled. Noonalook looked back out into the darkness where the cat had run. Facing Shokona and dying is what he'd wanted only the day before, but now he had to care for Sundu and get him back to his tribe. The boy would die out here without his help. Noonalook would have to postpone his death until he had completed his mission.

Sundu moved his bedding around to the other side of the fire, where he lay between the flames and Noonalook. Noonalook built the fire up then sat back. He watched Sundu until the boy fell asleep, thinking about what had happened and wondering if the cat had moved out here or if it had been following them.

Noonalook remembered the first time he saw Shokona after the attack, and it was also the first time he had been able to walk. He had gone alone in the forest to look for firewood. A twig snapped, and he turned to find Shokona hiding and watching him. He'd thought the cave lion had died after the battle, but the stab wounds Noonalook had inflicted had been slowly healing. He and Shokona locked eyes.

"Shokona," said Noonalook.

He dropped the wood and raised his arms in surrender to show the great cat he would not fight him. He tilted his head back and closed his eyes, waiting for Shokona to end his misery and reunite him with his family.    When nothing happened after a few moments, Noonalook opened his eyes to find Shokona gone.

"Shokona!" Noonalook said, but there was no sign of the lion.

He kept watch for nearly an hour and decided Shokona would not return. He threw more wood on the fire, then lay down. He thought it best not to tie anything to his leg again.

# FIVE

The morning sun had finally climbed over the mountains on the horizon, bathing them in bright, golden light as they followed the dewy trail. Crows jumped into the air and flew overhead, cawing angrily for being disturbed.

Noonalook looked back to make sure Sundu was following. The boy still carried his turtles, one in each hand, and straggled about 50 steps behind. Sundu's legs were short, and he grew tired quickly, and Noonalook was thankful for the frequent breaks. They had already stopped two times that morning to rest. Noonalook's right leg had bothered him yesterday, and today it was stiff and ached with each step. He found himself leaning more and more on his spear to help ease the pain. He had not walked this far since before his injury. Being dragged by Shokona had hurt his good leg, so now both legs gave him trouble.

As he looked back, he could see the trail they had made through the dew, leading far back to the trees where they'd stayed the night. It was barely visible now, and the forest where he lived was just a speck in the blue haze of the horizon.

Ahead, it appeared to Noonalook that he and Sundu would be leaving the prairie soon. Over the miles before them, the land gradually lost its flatness to gentle, rolling hills. Farther ahead, small mountains rose with patches of bare rock at their tops.

Noonalook had cooked the badger early that morning and carried most of it in his bag. They had eaten only a small portion of the badger for breakfast and would try to make the rest last until tomorrow. They had drunk all of the water, and Noonalook hoped there would be water in the hills ahead of them.

As they left the prairie and climbed up one of the short hills, they saw four woolly rhinoceroses grazing below. Noonalook quickly dropped to the ground below the waist-high grass and pulled Sundu down with him. Sundu stood back up to see what had frightened Noonalook and found the giant beasts.

"Stemma?" Sundu asked.

"Ahh?" asked Noonalook with questioning eyes and shook his head as if Sundu were crazy. He pulled the boy back down.

Noonalook knew one rhinoceros was dangerous enough to try to kill, even with every man in the tribe contributing. These animals were massive and aggressive. He had seen more than one man gored to death by the terrible horn on their noses.

Noonalook studied the wind, letting his face determined that it blew from the west, and the herd was to the north of them. He peeked back up over the grass and found the animals hadn't moved. That told Noonalook the rhinoceroses hadn't seen them or picked up their scent, and he sat back down. He didn't want to wait for them to leave, and he definitely didn't want to be discovered by them. They would have to sneak around the rhinoceroses carefully.

Noonalook put his hand to Sundu's mouth for him to be quiet, then gestured to keep low, and crawled away from Sundu in the tall grass. After a few feet, he waved for Sundu to follow. They crept slowly and quietly down the side of the hill. At the bottom, Noonalook peeked over the grass, making sure they were going in the right direction and check that the animals hadn't discovered them yet. He found the rhinoceroses still undisturbed and grazing.

Crawling through the tall, rough grass was tougher than Noonalook had at first imagined. His knees were scratched almost raw, and putting his weight down on his bad arm hurt. As Noonalook pushed through the grass, a long, black snake slithered toward him.

"Gahh!" Noonalook whispered in fright. He scrambled out of the way as it passed him. He noticed Sundu was not paying attention to anything other than one foot in front of the other as he walked hunched down below the grass. "Psst, Sundu!" Noonalook whispered.

Sundu looked up to see the snake slithering toward him. He screamed and stood up, dancing out of the snake's way. He had forgotten about the rhinoceroses.

"Psst! Na! Na!" Noonalook whispered, trying to get Sundu to hide again, but Sundu didn't move. His eyes were locked on to the rhinoceroses.

Noonalook raised his head up enough to see over the grass. All four rhinoceroses stared at Sundu. The bull scraped his foot on the ground and swung its head from side to side. Noonalook had seen that behavior before. The rhinoceroses were going to charge at Sundu. Noonalook thought that if he could frighten the rhinoceroses, maybe they would run away.

Noonalook stood quickly, waving his arms and spear, and yelled. The rhinoceroses saw Noonalook and ran away, except for one. Noonalook jumped up and down and shouted, but the bull rhinoceros only shook its head and snorted, becoming angrier. It kicked and scratched at the ground again, stirring up the dirt in the wind, then grunted and charged at Noonalook.

Noonalook ran, drawing the rhinoceros away from Sundu. When the other rhinoceroses saw the bull chasing the old man, they turned back and joined the chase.

Small trees, dotted sparsely about the hills, were the only place Noonalook could find shelter. The bull rhinoceros quickly caught up to Noonalook and only lagged a few yards behind. Beneath Noonalook's feet, the ground vibrated as the distance between him and the rhinoceros decreased. Noonalook spotted a small tree ahead of him and ran to it with the rhinoceros only a few feet behind and gaining. He could hear and feel the angry, slobbery snorts puffing from the beast on his back.

Noonalook reached out his good arm toward the small tree and hooked it as he ran by, swinging himself around the tree. The rhinoceros bashed the side of the tree as it ran by, bending it and knocking Noonalook down. He looked up in time to see the other three rhinoceroses running straight at him. He had just enough time to climb the tiny tree as the rhinoceroses blasted by, each one slamming the side of the tree. The trunk was barely thicker than Noonalook's arm, and it could not take such abuse.

The rhinoceroses circled around the tree, with each one striking it with their horns and massive bodies. The tree shook so hard Noonalook could hardly hang onto it. The tree trunk cracked, and the top swayed one way and then another as rhinoceroses inadvertently snapped the small tree in half. The tree fell over with a crash, and Noonalook lay still under its branches and leaves. He watched as the rhinoceroses pushed and hit the tree with their horns, scratched the ground, and snorted.

After some time, the rhinoceroses grew bored with the tree and seemed to forget what they had been chasing. They soon lost interest in the fallen tree, and the three rhinos slowly walked away. The bull rhinoceros scooted close to the tree and peed on it, then kicked the dirt and grass backward with its hind legs, and followed the others.

When they had gone, Noonalook quietly and painfully crawled out from under the tree. He wiped some of the pee from his face and grunted. He bled from all the scratches and scrapes over his body, and his hides were wet with urine. He found his spear and leaned on it heavily as he walked back to the hill. Sundu ran with the turtles to Noonalook. Noonalook didn't say anything but only waved for the boy to follow as he passed by.

It was late afternoon, and they had gotten closer to the rocky terrain where the hills became much steeper. It seemed they had been steadily walking uphill for hours. Noonalook's walk had slowed considerably since the rhinoceros attack. His bad leg had stiffened significantly, making each step excruciating.

Before them, they found a forest growing in a steep valley with cliffs and walls of rock leading to the valley floor. At the bottom of the valley, a river snaked through a wide gap in the forest. He hoped to make it to the river before dark. Clouds had been forming in the west all afternoon, and it would soon be dark earlier than usual.

They began their descent through the rocky region down into the valley where giant boulders and vertical rock walls towered over them. The thickening clouds and the forest canopy overhead made following the path much harder in the subdued light. Noonalook worried the trail would be difficult to follow through this rocky terrain, and if it rained, he could lose the path completely. He stopped and knelt to look for human tracks. There were subtle clues of broken twigs and stems and small, overturned rocks. These few traces of evidence here and there gave him hope he was still following them.

As they got closer to the valley floor, Noonalook smiled when he heard running water somewhere through the trees. Thunder rumbled overhead, and Noonalook and Sundu both looked up instinctively only to see the sky blocked by trees.

"Mubben," Sundu said, pointing up to a cliff.

Noonalook turned to where Sundu pointed, finding a cave in the face of the cliff. He studied the trail and saw that it led up to the cave. He looked back at Sundu and pointed toward the sound of the river. "Duntoo," he told Sundu and continued on down to the water. Sundu followed wearily behind.

Even in the darkness, it was easy to see the river was clear and swift. Sundu dropped near the edge and drank, but Noonalook wandered up and down the river's edge, studying the pebbles along the river bank. He found the rocks mostly undisturbed as he made his way slowly along the riverbank. Farther downstream, the stones had been displaced and scattered about. He walked to it and found the river shallow there. This is where Sundu's tribe had crossed the river. He knelt down to drink and filled the two bladders. When he had finished, he walked back to Sundu pointed up to where they had seen the cave.

"Mubben?" asked Sundu.

Noonalook nodded, not sure what the word meant, but assumed it probably meant "cave," and climbed up the steep hill. The growing darkness made it difficult to find safe places to step. Noonalook smelled the damp air coming from the cave above them. He also caught whiffs of human urine and excrement, which meant the tribe had recently stayed in the cave or someone lived there now.

Noonalook prepared himself as they approached the cave, should the occupants be unwelcoming or even hostile. He put his hand against Sundu's chest for him to stay. Sundu understood. Noonalook checked the knife in his belt and gripped the spear tightly, then crept quietly up to the cave. No firelight came from the cave, nor did the smell of smoke. When he reached the mouth of the cave, he strained to see inside through the darkness.

"Shudolla?" Noonalook called out. He heard nothing but his own voice echoing in the cave.

"Shundolla?" he called louder. No one answered. If there were no people inside, there could still be animals. He inched closer and closer inside the cave and squeezed his spear so tightly, his hands hurt.

His eyes adjusted somewhat to the darkness, but he could only see a few feet into the cave. At his feet were the blackened remains of a fire. He knelt down and put his hand near the burned wood and felt warmth. He stood up and pushed one of the logs over with his foot. Tiny, orange embers fell and burned out. If this fire had been from Sundu's tribe, they hadn't been gone long, possibly since that morning. There was even a small pile of unburned wood left in the cave. He walked back out and looked down at Sundu.

"Sundu, tooga," he said, motioning for the boy to join him. Sprinkles fell sporadically around them.

Sundu climbed into the cave as Noonalook removed the packs and set them down. He picked up a couple of sticks and showed them to Sundu then pointed outside. Sundu nodded and left his turtles upside down on the cave floor and ran out to gather more firewood. They would need only a little more to get them through the night, but they would need it before the wood became soaked from the rain.

Noonalook got to his knees and rolled the warm wood to where the charred area faced up. He blew on the log, and the blackened area glowed a dull red. It would be easy to make a fire tonight. He put some dried, crushed leaves and small twigs on the embers and blew on the log. After a few seconds, a flame flashed to life, and he added a few more sticks. He wasn't sure what he and Sundu would eat that night, though. They had eaten most of the badger throughout the day, and now he couldn't hunt or fish in the dark. Lightning flashed outside, and a few seconds later, thunder rumbled. The storm was moving closer.

As the fire grew, giving more light, Noonalook could see that the cave was not very deep, but it would keep the coming rain off of them and keep them warm. On the floor, he saw bones from small animals and fish scattered about. On the cave walls were handprints of people that had been there before and crude drawings of people and animals.

Noonalook saw the turtles trying to turn themselves upright and decided they would make a small but tasty meal for the night. He was sure the boy was tired of carrying them anyway. He took out his flint knife and cut the bottom shells off of them, then set the two upper halves next to the fire like bowls.

Sundu entered the cave a few minutes later with a large pile of firewood. As he neared the fire, he noticed the two dead turtles cooking. He dropped the wood and screamed. Startled, Noonalook fell backward, then jumped to his feet, pulling out his knife, and looked for the cause of the boy's screen.

"Oendoo hendi," Sundu screamed and pointed at the turtles.

Noonalook was confused. Sundu ran to Noonalook with tears in his eyes and beat on the old man with his fists. "Oendoo hendi!" the boy said again.

Noonalook tried to fend off the little fists as they struck blow after blow, and he pushed Sundu back. Sundu looked up at Noonalook with hatred and tears in his eyes then ran outside.

Noonalook stood stunned for a moment, trying to figure out what had just happened. He looked back at the turtles. Maybe the boy had kept the turtles as something to play with instead of eating.

The lightning flashed, and thunder boomed immediately after, bringing Noonalook back from his thoughts. The rain poured outside now. He had to go out and find the boy before he ended up lost in the dark or hurt. He put his knife back in his belt, picked up the spear, and hobbled outside.

The rain fell harder, and the thunder and lightning came more frequently. Noonalook took advantage of the flashes of light, but couldn't see Sundu anywhere. He walked back down the hill toward the river, slipping from the wet leaves and grass and falling a few times. The rain was cold, and the blowing wind made it colder. When he reached the bottom of the hill, he still couldn't find the boy and made his way to the river.

"Sundu!" he shouted, then listened the best he could through the noise of the storm, but he didn't hear a reply. He shivered in the cold as he looked around. It looked like the river had risen, carrying leaves, sticks, and other debris quickly downstream. He pulled the wet hair back from his eyes and ears, looking up and down the riverbank then back up toward the cave. "Sundu!" The boy wasn't here, and Noonalook hoped he hadn't fallen the river.

Noonalook walked back to the bottom of the steep hill under the cave. The cold rain encouraged him to wait for Sundu in the dry cave near the fire, but fear of the boy lost in the storm ate at his insides. He couldn't leave the boy alone outside all night, even if Sundu didn't want to stay with him anymore. He climbed back up toward the cave, hoping the boy had already returned when he heard Sundu scream. Noonalook froze, trying to determine the direction of the scream. "Sundu?" he called out.

Sundu screamed again, and Noonalook climbed in the direction of the cry.

He scrambled past the cave and found a large, flat ledge with a high rock wall against the hill. Sundu had backed into the wall with two, enormous, but thin, wolves creeping toward him. They moved low to the ground, with their backs hunched, and they growled through snarls. The position of their bodies indicated they were ready to strike at any time.

"Yahh!" shouted Noonalook as he waved his arms.

He surprised the wolves, but they didn't flee as he had hoped they would. One wolf kept his eyes on Noonalook while the other edged closer to Sundu. The wolves had found easy prey and were not going to be frightened off. Noonalook raised his spear and ran to the wolves. He knew if he didn't kill them both, one would go after the boy.

The spearhead caught the first wolf in the shoulder, but it yelped and jumped away. Noonalook stabbed at the other wolf, and it sprang back, allowing Noonalook to get between Sundu and the wolves. He motioned for Sundu to climb up the rock wall. The boy would be safe there for a while.

The wolves moved in closer, showing their teeth. Sundu scaled up the wall just above Noonalook's head and out of the wolves' reach.

"Yahh!" Noonalook yelled again.

The wolves did not flinch this time.

Noonalook tightened the grip on his spear and shifted his eyes from wolf to wolf, looking for any aggressive movement that would lead to an attack. Sundu was safe for now, but if Noonalook tried to climb up too, they would attack him from behind. It appeared the wolves were not going to back down. Hunger controlled their ferocity and persistence. Noonalook knew that any fear he felt would be sensed by the wolves, and that would trigger an attack.

Noonalook took a small step forward, but they did not back away and held their ground. He saw he had hurt the first wolf from the blood staining the fur on its shoulder. He would go after the uninjured one first. It would be difficult to get a good hit on the wolf unless he went for its back or side. He stepped closer, and both wolves crouched lower, ready to spring.

The lightning flashed, and Noonalook ran to the uninjured wolf and thrust the spear into its side. The wolf cried out and bit and snapped at the spear handle. Noonalook pushed with all his strength against the thrashing wolf, driving the spear in deeper. The other wolf seized the opportunity of Noonalook's distraction and jumped on his back, snapping at Noonalook's neck, and they both fell to the ground.

"Noonalook!" Sundu cried out.

Noonalook lay on the ground as the wolf bit his shoulders and back, trying to reach his neck. Noonalook was smart enough to keep his shoulders hunched up to protect his neck. The bites were painful on his shoulders, head, and back as the wolf tore into his flesh, digging for a death hold on Noonalook's neck.

Noonalook reached out to grab the spear, but the dying wolf staggered away, dragging the spear with it, and fell down. As Noonalook stretched out his hand towards spear, the wolf on his back dug its teeth into the back of Noonalook's neck. Noonalook grabbed at his knife, but it was pinned beneath his body. The wolf clenched his fangs deeper into Noonalook's neck, and he felt his left arm go numb. The wolf was going to kill him. He couldn't die now, he still had to see the boy safely back to his tribe.

Noonalook tried to hit the wolf, but couldn't reach back far enough. He tried to crawl away, but the weight of the wolf pinned him down. He tried again for the knife in his belt. He rolled to his left to pull it from his right side. He managed to get it out of his belt, but dropped it, finding his right hand was now weak and also going numb. He blindly felt for the knife on the ground and grabbed it again. This time he held on as tightly as he could and stabbed the air behind him, but couldn't reach the wolf. Noonalook grew weaker by the second and wondered if he would live long enough for the boy to at least get back to the cave.

Noonalook pushed with his legs against the ground and used his weight to roll over on his back. The wolf immediately went for Noonalook's exposed throat. Noonalook blocked the wolf's attack with his left arm by pushing it into the wolf's mouth, then stabbed the knife into the animal's side. The wolf jumped away. There was blood rage in the wolf's eyes.

Noonalook's left arm had been chewed up, reminding him of the similar defensive technique he'd used against Shokona. His right hand was sticky with the wolf's blood, and his left arm was sticky with his own blood. He knew he had hurt the wolf, but he didn't know if it would be enough to escape.

Noonalook sat up, pointing the bloody knife at the wolf as he tried to stand. Before he could straighten up, his knees buckled, and he fell back to the rocky surface with a sudden and overwhelming desire to sleep.

The wolf sensed the weakness in the old man and had tasted his blood. It slowly stalked closer. Noonalook pushed himself to stand, but his legs could not support him, and he fell again. He found the weight of the knife in his hand, getting so heavy he could hardly hold it up as the wolf inched closer.

# SIX

Sundu screamed, and Noonalook looked up in time to see a massive, dark figure jump from above Sundu's head onto the wolf. Noonalook squinted to see what it was. It wasn't a man; it was another animal. A large animal.

Noonalook didn't know if he was dreaming or if this was really happening. There was a vicious fight between the beasts. He fought to keep his eyes open. He wanted to find out what was happening, but the desire to sleep was strong. He had to sleep. The rain. The cold rain. The water felt good, splashing on him, soaking him, washing him away, bit by bit.

Something grabbed and pulled his arm. He opened his eyes and found Sundu pulling him to stand. Had he fallen asleep? He wanted to sleep. There was the pull again. The pull to get up. To go. But he was so tired, so sleepy. Why should he have to go?

Sundu screamed something and pointed back to the animals. The lightning flashes revealed a cave lion's bloody jaws clenched around the dead wolf's neck. Cave lion? Noonalook stared at the puddled blood from the dead wolf. It looked black in the dark but thinned to little, dark clouds in the rain. There was the pull again. Go. He had to go.

Noonalook attempted to stand, but fell to his knees. When the lightning flashed again, Noonalook saw the cat clearly in the flashes of light. It was Shokona. The scars on the cat and the cat's staring eyes on Noonalook told him this was Shokona. Shokona?

Noonalook felt Sundu pulling him and heard his desperate pleading for him to move. Noonalook got to his feet, dizzy and unsteady. Sundu pulled Noonalook away from the cat and the wolves. The lion only stared at Noonalook and Sundu as they slowly backed away.

Noonalook stumbled down the side of the steep hill. He looked back once more to Shokona, but the cat was not there. Noonalook's foot caught on an exposed tree root, and he fell forward, leaving Sundu's grip. He felt the thick cushion of dead leaves, soaked with rain, and the hardness of the rocks as he fell into them. His body rolled and slid down the wet, slippery hill.

He woke and found himself on his feet again, stumbling about in the rain. Then, for a moment, he found himself climbing back up the hill.

He smelled smoke from the fire, the urine and the excrement from the cave, and his own blood.

There was light, then there was warmth. Noonalook opened his eyes to find the fire before him. He was lying down, but didn't remember lying down and didn't remember returning to the cave. He was on one of his furs, but couldn't recall pulling it close to the fire or how he came to be on top of it.

Sundu laid another skin over Noonalook. Noonalook looked up at the boy and smiled. His throat hurt, and the back of his neck and shoulders burned like fire. What was wrong with him? He was reminded of the aftermath of Shokona's deadly attack on him and his family years before. Confusion, the waking nightmares, and the sick, dreamy illusions and realities had all blended together in a disoriented horror. He seemed to be back there again.

The desire to sleep washed over him again, and he put his head down and slept.

Sundu threw more wood on the fire, then sat down next to Noonalook and cried.

Noonalook found himself standing in a green prairie with the sun shining brightly overhead. He looked around at the lush greens and dark blue sky and knew it was early summer. He seemed disoriented or maybe a little lost, but his surroundings seemed familiar to him. He couldn't remember where he had come from or how he had gotten there. He remembered being cold, but now he wasn't. The sun warmed the soothing breeze blowing across him. How was it that the sky had never seemed so blue before? Why was the air so fresh, and why did he feel so good?

Behind him was a forest he felt he should know. It took only a moment before he realized it was the forest of his village, and he walked to it. He noticed his leg did not hurt, and he did not limp. He looked down and found no injuries or scars on any part of his body. He wasn't even sure he had ever had scars or if he had ever limped. Why had he expected to see scars? He couldn't recall ever being hurt so severely or why he thought he had been.

He walked through the forest, not sure of his way, but felt drawn to the direction he traveled as if through instinct. Ahead, he saw his village, and as he progressed, he saw his wife, Shawnjee, preparing vegetation for a meal, and his son, Tondoe, playing with other boys. Noonalook's heart jumped when he saw them and felt an overwhelming excitement with the desperate urge to run. And he did run. He ran fast and light and wasn't out of breath just as he had been as a boy.

He swooped up Shawnjee, holding her close, and she laughed at his playfulness. He put her down and studied her, absorbing every detail of her face. He felt like crying but didn't know why. As his son ran by, chasing other children, Noonalook scooped him up and hugged him tightly. He felt the little arms of Tondoe reach around his neck and hug him back. Why did he feel like he hadn't seen his family for a long time? Why was he both happy and sad?

"Gundoo," said a voice behind him. He turned and saw three of the village men. Gundoo? He is not chief of the village anymore. Why did they call him that? Was he chief? He had vague notions that he was, or had been, why couldn't he remember? Was something wrong with him? He recognized the men from his village, but they were younger than he had remembered. Two of them were his friends he had grown up with, but for some strange reason, he thought one of them had died. The third man with them was much older than the other two and was the village shaman. Noonalook saw the holy man held paints for the sacred hunting markings, and he put Tondoe down.

Noonalook knelt before the old man. The holy man chanted magical words as he painted the markings on Noonalook's face. There was something he tried to remember about the sacred symbols and the magic words, but he couldn't recall what it was. Noonalook stood when the holy man had finished, and one of his friends handed him his spear.

"Shokona," his friend said.

Shokona? Could it really be Shokona? The large cave lion had recently been seen lurking about the perimeters of the village. Two hunting dogs had disappeared, and Shokona had gotten the blame. The people were afraid a child could be next. Noonalook had not seen the lion, but he somehow knew what it looked like as if he'd seen it in his dreams. He knew it was big and fierce, and he knew it was deadly. Someone in the village had named the great cat Shokona because it was the biggest cave lion anyone had ever seen.

Noonalook recognized two other men joining them. They told him they had spotted the lion not far from the village. Today was the day they were finally going to kill it, and Noonalook would lead the hunt.

Noonalook checked his spear, making sure the head was sharp and tightly attached to the handle, then he felt the knife at his side. The holy man chanted blessings on them as Noonalook led the men through the forest. Noonalook had the feeling that all of this was strangely familiar to him, but he wasn't sure why.

The forest darkened their surroundings. The green canopy overhead blocked a lot of the sunlight.

Small sparkles of sunshine danced on the ground in the otherwise continuous shade. Noonalook could tell the men were on edge as they crept around the trees and through the brush, looking for any signs of movement. Except for the rustle of leaves far above them and an occasional bird somewhere, the forest was eerily quiet, making the sounds of their feet crunching through the forest floor seem louder than usual. Noonalook's heart pounded in his chest. He felt an overwhelming and unwarranted fear that wanted to paralyze him. He couldn't let the other men know he had this fear. He had to show them strength.

No one saw or heard it until it was too late. The lion sprang from nowhere and clenched its teeth into the throat of one of the men, knocking him to the ground and nearly tearing off his head. Noonalook finally saw the lion that had seemed to visit his nightmares thousands of times.

The man in Shokona's mouth struggled for only a few seconds with his arms and legs flailing wildly in the air. The man tried to scream, but only produced airy, bloody gurgles. He writhed for a second more, then was still. Shokona dropped the dead man as the other men inched in closer. The lion paced about before the body, staring at the hunters. The man's blood, mixed with the lion's saliva, ran from its mouth and dripped from its whiskers.

Noonalook could see why this animal had been called Shokona. It was the largest lion he had ever seen, almost to the point of being a monster. Strong, tight muscles were visible throughout the lion's short, creamy gray fur. Noonalook had never known of another animal to act so aggressively toward a human. The only time he had ever seen an animal attack was when it had been injured or threatened, but Shokona had not been threatened or hurt. Could the large cat be smart enough to know they were hunting it? Noonalook watched the beast pace before the man's body. To Noonalook, it appeared that Shokona watched and waited for the next person who dared to approach. This was not a hunt anymore; it was a war.

Noonalook felt himself step forward as if controlled by someone else. He was aware of the three remaining men ready and waiting for the attack. Noonalook kept his eyes on the lion as it stopped pacing and faced him. The lion's eyes moved from man to man, each one studying the other, looking for any signs of a coming assault.

Shokona lunged quickly and unexpectedly. The lion hit Noonalook. Noonalook fell on his back, knocking the breath out of him. He tried to spear the lion but was not fast enough. Shokona swung the sharp claws at Noonalook's head. Noonalook held up the spear defensively, but the lion knocked it from Noonalook's hands. The next swipe brought the deadly paw down on Noonalook's head, ripping open part of his face and scalp. Then he felt the claws tear into his chest as if to dig out his heart. The other men rushed forward and stabbed the great cat with their spears. Shokona roared, curdling every man's blood, then shot off into the forest.

The men ran to Noonalook. They helped him stand wearily to his feet, and someone handed him his spear Noonalook pointed to the village.

"Punedaggo!" he said, barely more than a whisper, then ran the best he could, with the remaining men following their leader. Noonalook had a sense that the cat had run in the direction of their village. Shokona had been dangerous before, but now he was injured, and he would be even more vicious. "Punedaggo!" Noonalook said again. His plea was urgent.

By the time Noonalook and his men reached their village, an older man, a young woman, and two children lay bloody and dead on the ground, making a macabre trail to Shokona in the middle of the village where he had cornered some of the villagers standing before him. Shawnjee, two other women, and the holy man protected the other children with sticks and spears from the large lion. Shokona's head was low to the ground, scrutinizing the people as if determining which one would be next.

Noonalook saw Shawnjee motioning for him and wailing as he followed the trail of corpses. He had never seen Shawnjee behave that way, and a sense of urgency hurried him forward. As he approached the bodies of the children, horror rushed through him. One of the children was his son.

"Tondoe?" he said in disbelief. "Tondoe!"

He dropped the spear and fell to his knees over his son. He checked for signs of life but found none. The little boy had been sliced open from throat to groin. Noonalook turned back to the lion with tears of rage in his eyes. He grabbed his spear and charged. A guttural scream of hate bellowed up from deep inside Noonalook as he attacked the lion in a hellish fury.

"Bongla, Noonalook!" Shawnjee cried. She tried to run to him to help him, but the villagers held her back.

Noonalook stabbed the spear at the lion, but

the lion sprang up over Noonalook's head and landed behind him. Before Noonalook could turn around, Shokona jumped on Noonalook's back, knocking him down and sank its teeth into the back of Noonalook's neck and shoulder. His spear flew from his hands. He tried to reach it, but it was too far away. He pulled out his knife and stabbed the lion in its front shoulder, and the lion let him go. Noonalook scrambled away, but Shokona snatched him up by the leg with its sharp and jagged teeth, then shook its head fiercely, tearing flesh and muscle and breaking the bone in Noonalook's thigh.

Shawnjee broke free from the villagers and ran to the lion with the spear, but the lion saw her coming. He dropped Noonalook and swatted her down as if she were a doll. She was petite and barely 17 years old, and she didn't stand a chance. Shokona pounced on her, like a cat on a mouse. Noonalook heard ribs snapping beneath her skin, and within a split second, Shokona had ripped out her throat from chin to chest.

Noonalook couldn't believe what he had just seen. He was numb inside. He clumsily stood to his feet, holding tightly to the knife. Blood rushed to his ears, blocking all the sounds of the screams, growls, and cries, all but his own heartbeat. Tunnel vision formed in his eyes, and he saw nothing but Shokona. He didn't see the village men running to him to stop him. They grabbed for him, but he turned on them, swinging the knife and threatening them with it. Nothing was going to stop him. He turned back to the lion. Noonalook did not care anymore if he lived or died, as long as the lion died, too. Nothing else mattered in his life now but the death of Shokona.

Someone with nothing left to risk or lose, and nothing left in the world to live for can do mighty things. And he did a mighty thing.

Noonalook jumped on the lion's back as it was distracted by the village men and their spears. Noonalook held onto the lion skin with his left hand and stabbed as hard and as fast as he could with his right. Shokona flipped Noonalook from its back to the ground. Noonalook held off Shokona with his left arm, protecting his neck, as he continued to stab with his right hand. Noonalook felt and heard the bone in his left-hand snap between Shokona's jaws, but he felt no pain. The lion's blood mixed with his and dripped into Noonalook's face. The other men stabbed the lion with their spears. Shokona roared and swiped the deadly claws at them, then fled. The men chased after the lion until they could no longer see it, then returned to the village.

Noonalook was drenched in blood. He coughed up more blood and tried to get up but couldn't. He saw his wife's body near him. He managed to roll to his stomach, then pulled himself to her where he lay his head on her bloody stomach and moaned. "Shawnjee!"

The shaman stood over Noonalook then looked at the two men standing nearby. "Collun doe dedanto bole denaho," the shaman said to the men.

The two men each grabbed one of Noonalook's arms and dragged him into the holy man's shelter.

The shaman washed the blood away from Noonalook's face, revealing the faint sacred markings still there. The old man chanted his unique words and put particular leaves and stones on specific areas of

Noonalook's body and forehead. Noonalook thought of nothing but his family. Even the severe pain he suffered was shadowed by the heartbreak and loss that punished him. He didn't want the holy man to save him, he wanted to join his family in the other life where they waited for him.

The old shaman scooted away, busy with his magic objects. Noonalook heard him gathering the different magic and healing items somewhere behind him. The images of Shokona ripping out Shawnjee's throat and the exposed entrails of Tondoe had seared into his mind and replayed over and over. Why was he still living? How much longer did he have to suffer? He knew he could not live long with his injuries, no one could. He was excited to see his family again. All he had to do was just wait and die. He knew it would be soon. It had to be. Noonalook needed to tell the holy man to let him die. With such pain in his body and heart, he didn't want to live. "C... carto... carto de... on... onetta," Noonalook sputtered out.

"Carto de onetta, Noonalook?" the shaman asked.

"J… jinno," Noonalook said.

"Ahh?!" asked the holy man, surprised at the request. He returned to Noonalook with a burning torch for a better examination. "Jundolla de mundun?"

Noonalook tried to answer but couldn't.

"Jundolla de mundun?" the holy man asked again as he brought the bright torch closer to Noonalook, blinding him with the light. "Jundolla de mundun?"

Noonalook blinked at the sunlight shining in the cave and onto his face. For a moment he was disoriented and didn't know where he was until he tried to move and felt pain shoot through his body and then he remembered the attack. He remembered the wolves and Shokona and Sundu being in trouble, but he didn't remember returning to the cave.

He rested his head back and stared at the ceiling. The attack had brought back the torture of what Shokona had done those many years ago. He hated that dream, and he hated being reminded of that tragic day. Every time the nightmare returned, he always felt bad for a day or two afterward because he could not get it out of his mind. It lingered like an insect bite, irritating and itchy at first, and slowly fading away with time.

He tried to sit up, but his shoulder burned with pain, and he lay back down. The fire burned beside him, and more wood had been stacked inside. He didn't see the boy around, but someone had gathered firewood and kept the fire burning. The charred turtle shells near the fire were empty except for some bones. He didn't remember eating them.

He found his spear and knife laying nearby. Dried blood covered them both and had stained the wooden handle of the spear. They had been placed near him, but he knew he couldn't have done it.

He rolled over and finally sat up with a painful grunt. He felt dizzy and closed his eyes for a moment until the sensation had passed. Blood and dirt were caked across him, and his wounds were swollen and painful. He looked back outside. This was not early morning light, as he had first thought, but early afternoon light.

"Sundu?" he called out. His voice echoed inside the cave.

He put the knife in his belt, then pulled the spear close and used it to stand. He didn't know if Shokona was still out there somewhere, and he had to make sure the boy was okay.

He slowly walked to the mouth of the cave and looked out. The storm had knocked a lot of the dead leaves and limbs from the trees. In the river below, Sundu splashed about in the cold water chasing a fish. The inexperience and awkwardness of the boy trying to catch the fish made Noonalook smile.

Noonalook slowly climbed down from the cave, looking about for the lion, but never saw him. Each movement of his shoulder and arm was excruciating.

Using his spear as a cane, he reached the valley floor and walked to the river. He stood on the bank until Sundu noticed him.

"Noonalook!" Sundu said with a smile on his face.

He ran out of the water and hugged Noonalook, then turned back to the river and pointed.

"Oendoo," he said.

Noonalook smiled at him and walked into the cold river with his spear. The boy stood on the bank to watch.

Noonalook stood patiently in the river with his spear ready and the tip just under the water. His legs stung in the freezing current, and soon his feet became numb. Fish swam and darted about, curious about the man's legs, but they were all too small to eat. Noonalook knew a bigger one would come eventually, and he waited.

He finally spotted a large fish swimming lazily about. He wiggled his big toe until the fish saw it. The fish moved in for a closer investigation. Noonalook matched the fish's movement with his spear as he cleverly moved it closer to the fish. He wiggled his toe again to distract the fish, then stabbed it. He swung the spear up out of the water, revealing the impaled fish.

Sundu jumped up and down on the river bank and shouted with joy. Noonalook threw the spear and fish on the river bank near Sundu. He then washed his wounds and removed the dried blood. The freezing water took his breath away, but it felt good to get the sticky blood off.

He ambled out of the water and sat on the bank near the fish, and Sundu sat beside him.

"Dena Shokona?" asked Noonalook.

He pantomimed the cave lion using his fingers like claws and hissed.

"Hendi," said Sundu, shaking his head.

Shokona's behavior made no sense to Noonalook. He and Sundu had traveled so far, and the lion had followed them, but why had he followed them? Why didn't Shokona kill them instead of the wolf? Shokona had ample opportunity as they slept in the cave. Even though there was no sign of him, Noonalook felt Shokona was still about, hiding somewhere and watching them.

He shook his head to make the thoughts go away so he could concentrate on the fish. Noonalook took out his knife and cleaned the fish slowly and carefully, demonstrating to Sundu how to do it. When he had finished, Noonalook threw the guts into the water, and he and Sundu hiked back up to the cave.

The sun had moved farther above the hills and no longer warmed the cave with its light as they sat near the fire and ate the fish. Noonalook knew it would not be wise to travel this late in the day when they already had a shelter, a fire, and water nearby. They would leave out early in the morning. He was sure the rain had washed the trail away, and he would need the sunlight to look for left-over traces of it.

After they finished eating, Noonalook and Sundu climbed back up to where Sundu's encounter with the wolves had been. Noonalook had to see it again and see if there were any clues to Shokona's strange ways.

The dead wolves were still there, but the stomachs of both wolves had been eaten by something big, probably Shokona. Sundu stood back as Noonalook walked about the carcasses, studying them.

It was strange that the bones and muscles were still intact, but the innards were gone entirely. The large predators, like Shokona, would rip away and break the bones. They wasted nothing. Smaller animals and insects had been busy on the soft parts of the wolves, such as the eyes and tongue, but most of the wolves were still there and only partially eaten. And there were flies. That's when Noonalook realized the wolves had not been killed last night, but probably two nights ago. The flies could not have found them this quickly. He must have been hurt worse than he thought and slept longer than just one night.

He looked back at Sundu, who'd gotten brave enough to poke one of the dead wolves with a stick and realized Sundu had been hungry, and that's why the turtles had been eaten, and he had been trying to catch a fish.

It was a shame to not eat the meat or take the hides of the wolves, he could have used both, but the two animals had been dead for too long. There was nothing more to see here. Noonalook motioned for Sundu to follow, and they returned to the cave.

Noonalook put more wood on the fire and laid back down on the skins. Sundu sat beside him and patted his head. Noonalook smiled and closed his eyes.

The chilly wind blew into the cave, waking Noonalook and making him shiver. It was dark outside, and the fire had gotten low. He found Sundu was asleep close by and near the fire. He painfully sat up and added more wood. A small pile of walnuts and a full bladder of water lay near where Noonalook had slept. The boy had been concerned for him. He cracked the nuts open and ate them and drank from the bladder. He felt sleepy again and laid back down and was soon asleep.

Cawing crows outside the cave woke Noonalook early the next morning before the sun had risen. Sundu still slept, curled up like a dog under the fur to keep warm. Noonalook quietly got up, taking the spear and knife with him, and left the cave.

Noonalook made his way down to the bottom of the hill, hoping to find more food before traveling, and the best place for that was the river. He waded into the freezing, swift current and waited with the spearhead slightly below the surface. His legs ached in the cold water, then they felt as if they were burning, then he felt nothing in his legs.

It took nearly an hour to catch two fish, but they were big enough to fill their bellies, and Noonalook was glad to get out of the numbing water. He sat on the bank and rested for a moment. The continuous shivering had made him tired, and he knew he wouldn't stop shivering until he returned to the fire. He quickly cleaned the fish then climbed back up to the cave.

Sundu stirred awake and sat up, wrapping the skin tightly around himself. He watched through sleepy eyes as Noonalook rigged two sticks with the fish on them then hung over the fire. As the fish cooked, Noonalook gathered and packed their things. He left Sundu with the fur and gave him a little more time to wake up. He knew the boy had been through a lot lately.

Up and down the riverbank, Noonalook searched for any signs of the trail but found none. He looked back up at the cave then back across the river, searching for the most likely way the tribe could have traveled. Without the crow-head peak or a path, he had nothing to go on except a guess based on his own experience.

The steep hills and boulders they either had to crawl over or find a way around, made their morning journey difficult. Noonalook continuously searched for any evidence of human activity, but the storm had washed everything away. He wondered what would happen if he never could find the tribe. While following a clear and distinct path, the thought had never crossed his mind. He was pretty sure he could find his way back to his own village, but the boy was not wanted there, and, really, neither was he. He could take care of Sundu for a few years and teach him everything he needed to know to survive, but the boy would need other people, and soon, he would want a wife.

Noonalook considered finding another tribe, a friendly but powerful tribe, and try to get them to take the boy in. If he could teach Sundu everything he knew, it would make the boy valuable to the tribe, and they would be more willing to take him. He knew no one would take a useless and scarred old man, and he would once again be on his own.

The farther Noonalook and Sundu traveled from the river, the flatter the ground once again became. They didn't make much progress that day, and they stopped early when they came across a grove of apple trees. The day's journey had worn Noonalook out, and he was thankful he didn't have to hunt this night.

Sticks and broken branches littered the ground beneath the apple trees, and gathering firewood was effortless that night. Noonalook worked with a ball of dried grass and leaves and twigs to get a fire started. His shoulder burned with pain as he worked to get even the smallest whisk of smoke. Once the flames burned steadily, Noonalook cleaned an area around the fire and laid out the skins. He sat down and fed the campfire with the wood within arm's reach while he ate a couple of the sweet apples. Sundu piled enough firewood to last them through the night and explained to Noonalook that he had found water also.

Before dark, Sundu led Noonalook to the

little stream he had found. The croaking frogs quieted as they approached, leaving only the sound of the trickling of water over rocks. The stream was too small for large fish, but schools of minnows swam about. As they drank, Sundu spotted a big turtle crawling under the water. He reached in to pull it out, but it bit his hand and wouldn't let go. Sundu screamed as he tried to pull his hand away from the turtle's jaws.

Noonalook jumped into the stream and pulled the heavy and slippery snapping turtle out of the water and carefully led Sundu and the turtle to dry land. He tried to work the mouth open, but its bite was too strong.

Noonalook pulled out his knife and cut the turtle's head off, but it still didn't release Sundu. He worked the stone blade carefully into the turtle's mouth and pried out Sundu's bloody hand. Noonalook washed the wound in the stream and examined it. The flesh had torn where the turtle had clenched on, and it would be sore for a few days.

Noonalook picked up the turtle by its knobby, pointed tail. "Stemma?" he asked.

Sundu glared at the turtle. "Stemma."

The night had come, and the turtle cooked upside down in the coals near the fire. The lower shell had been removed, and the upper carapace was used as a pot. Noonalook had poured some water in to make a soup and added bits of apple, filling the air with a musky, sweet smell.

Noonalook quietly sang softly as he stirred and poked the bits of meat and apple around with a stick. It had been a long time since he had been so lighthearted and didn't realize he was singing until Sundu joined in. Noonalook stopped his song and didn't know why he had even begun. Sundu stopped too and looked at Noonalook to see what was wrong. It seemed odd to Noonalook that he could find no reason to sing, but he also couldn't think of a reason to not sing. He looked back at Sundu, studying him and remembered the boy crying over his dead father. Noonalook smiled and sang again. Sundu smiled when he saw there was nothing wrong and sang along with Noonalook.

# SEVEN

The frogs had sung their songs all through the night but had grown quiet at dawn. Preparing for their journey, Noonalook filled his bag with apples. Sundu quietly sat and watched, not quite fully awake. They drank from the stream and filled their containers with fresh water before setting out.

Pink and purple colored the sky and clouds as they stumbled and dodged the rocks. In the dim light, the rocky land gradually turned into what looked like a prairie and farther beyond we're the mountains. The crow-head peak glowed orange against the violet sky as the sun's rays struck it first. The summit had changed its shape a little as they had gotten closer, but it still kept its recognizable form. Noonalook made the crow-head peak their destination if they did not pick up the tribe's trail again.

There had been a dew during the night, and the moisture on the traveler's feet and legs chilled them. Noonalook knew it wouldn't be long before the dew became frost, then the frost becomes snow.

Traveling alone back to his tribe during winter frightened him, but it was beginning to look like he may not have a choice.

The cave they had stayed in a few nights before would be the best place to stay through the winter. It would be warmer than his little hut, with a good water supply and plenty of wood, but he would be alone. It was true he had no friends or family back in the village, and even though no one spoke to him or ever treated him kindly, any human presence was better than none.

All of his problems would be solved if he could only find the boy's tribe. He would make it back home before winter, and he wouldn't have to think about his future anymore.

Noonalook glanced back at Sundu, walking sleepily behind him and occasionally stumbling over a rock. Noonalook had noticed the boy did not like to get up early. When Sundu became a man, he would have to learn to be up before the sun to provide food for his family and village.

Noonalook couldn't recall if he were as reluctant to get out of bed as Sundu when he had been that young. He had hunted and fished with his father since he could remember, and those had always taken place at predawn. He didn't have many memories from that long ago, but there were two he would never forget. The first was his father beating him, and the second was when his father had died.

There were scant recollections of ever playing with the other boys in the village or having fun, but the memory of the time he got hit in the head with a stone and vomited afterward was strong. His father had beat him for wasting food, and he wasn't allowed to eat anything until the next day.

The day his father died from a snake bite had always stuck with him. It was the day Noonalook became a man. He had been only a few years old than Sundu was now when he took on the responsibility of providing food for himself and his mother.

Having been thrown into the position of being a man at such an early age gave him a lot of experience. Noonalook knew that was the reason he had been given the role of the leader in the village. When the former chief had grown too old to hunt for the tribe anymore, he gave the leadership to Noonalook.

During the celebration of Noonalook's new authority, one man opposed the chief's decision. The man, quite a few years older than Noonalook, believed he should have been the rightful owner of the position. The man was angry and jealous of Noonalook and challenged him to be chief.

Noonalook was only a scared teenager who had no experience with fighting men. Being challenged for the position made Noonalook angry with the man for questioning his ability and the chief's endorsement. When he accepted the challenge, they fought with their knives. Noonalook was thin and fast, and he won the title that day. When he killed the man, it felt so different than killing an animal. The death of an animal provided food, tools, and skins. The death of a person provided nothing.

Noonalook had backed away from the dead man as the wife and children ran to the body and cried. He felt terrible for the family left behind, and he hated himself for having to kill the man, but he couldn't show any weakness. He left the village to wash his hands in the stream and cried harder for that man than he did for his own father.

"Iktchi," said Sundu.

Noonalook snapped from his memories back to the present. Sundu pointed to something on the ground. Noonalook walked back to see what the boy had found. It was human excrement, possibly a day old. Looking about for other signs of the trail, he found broken patches of grass, and knelt. As he looked closer, human footprints were imprinted in the bare spots of soil. He followed with his eyes to where the footprints led and was surprised to find they headed to the west. The tribe had been traveling north this whole time. Noonalook stood, scratching his head, and wondered why they had changed direction. The river they had crossed the day before appeared to run from the west. Why would anyone give up the resources of the river and come all the way out here only to travel west? It made no sense to Noonalook, but if that's the way the people went, then he and Sundu would have to follow. He turned their direction to the west and followed the trail.

Toward mid-morning, the ground became uneven with stones jutting from the surface. It seemed they had just left the rocky terrain to only return to it again. Noonalook hated the thought of having to traverse through the rough land again. There were more mountains ahead, but they were much farther away. Noonalook glanced back to the north at the crow-head peak, and already it had become distorted and harder to recognize as they angled away from it.

They neared a rocky area that dropped off into a valley with only the tops of the trees showing.

Noonalook froze when he heard voices coming from somewhere ahead of them in the valley. He crouched down and crept closer to the edge with Sundu low and following.

Noonalook's hopes were high that they had finally caught up with the tribe, but he wanted to be careful before showing himself and getting killed. They crawled to the edge and peeked over the side. Below, seven men with spears sat on rocks and talked. Noonalook turned to Sundu and pointed to the men below. He could only remember one word Sundu had said, and that was for mother.

"Dendaya?" Noonalook asked.

Sundu looked to Noonalook with fear in his eyes and shook his head. "Hendi," he said.

Noonalook looked back at the men below with a sick feeling when he acknowledged that they had followed the wrong tribe. Now he knew why the trail had abruptly and unexpectedly cut to the west. But where were their women and children? It looked like a hunting party, but if this was a hunting party, why were the men sitting down? This didn't make any sense. Then the low sound of thunder rumbled.

He and Sundu looked up and didn't see a single cloud in the sunny sky, but the thunder grew louder, and the ground vibrated. Down below, the men also heard the thundering, and they sprang to action with their spears ready. Noonalook now knew what the men were doing. He looked behind them to discover a heard of bison stampeding toward them.

Noonalook grabbed Sundu by the back of his skins and dragged him as he dashed to get away from the bison's deadly path. They raced from the ravine's edge to the safety of a pile of boulders, hid behind them, and watched.

More men chased the bison on foot, shouting and waving their spears, pushing the beasts in a blind panic toward the edge of the ravine. The bison ran over the side, tumbling over one another. Legs and necks broke, and the younger ones were trampled to death. The bison that survived all the way to the bottom ran past the waiting men. Once the animals were gone, the men ran to the injured animals and killed them. The men that had chased the bison joined their tribesmen and helped kill and butcher. They cut and took what they could carry, then climbed up the ravine to take their loads back to their village. Two men remained behind to protect their kills from scavengers until the others could come back.

Noonalook and Sundu sneaked back to the ravine's edge and watched as the two men left behind gathered wood and built a fire. One of the men cut off large portions from one of the bison and roasted it over the fire. Noonalook wanted some of the meat for himself and the boy, but he didn't think those men would just let him have some, so he would have to sneak in and steal it.

He motioned for Sundu to stay, and he ran low to the ground along the rim. He stopped and lay down where the bison had run over the side and crawled to the edge. The men below hadn't seen him and still talked as they cooked their food. The closest bison to Noonalook was a trampled, dead calf about halfway down the incline. The grass was nearly tall enough to conceal Noonalook as he slowly crept to the calf.

He checked to make sure he had not been

discovered, then looked back at the top of the canyon where Sundu's head appeared over the top of one of the boulders, watching him. Noonalook took out his knife and cut into the calf's leg. The calf screamed. Noonalook immediately dropped close to the ground behind the calf and lay motionless as it kicked its legs and wailed.

The men stood and looked about, trying to find the bison making the noise. There were a few calves scattered across the ravine wall, but only one was kicking and bawling. Noonalook peeked over the calf to find the two men climbing toward him. He didn't want to fight for the meat, but now he would have to fight for his and Sundu's lives. He took a deep breath and gripped the knife, readying himself when a movement above him caught his eye. Sundu quickly stood and threw a rock where it hit near the fire. The men looked back down to see what had made the noise.

Noonalook took advantage of the situation and slit the calf's throat. It kicked a few more times, then lay still and quiet. Noonalook watched as the two men looked back at the fire, then back up the hill. The crying had stopped, so they returned to their cooking meat.

Noonalook cut into the calf, taking an entire back leg and a lot of the meat surrounding it. Below, the men were distracted with their food, allowing Noonalook to escape. He carefully and quietly crawled back up to the top, and away from the edge, dragging the calf leg with him. Sundu met him, and they ran, following the bloody trail the hunters had left as they returned to their tribe. Noonalook carried the meat with the cut part hanging down, letting the blood drain and mix with the blood splatter on the path.

After traveling about a mile, Noonalook diverted from following the hunters to make a confusing trail over and around rocks then circled back to where they'd started. Noonalook knew once the men had found a partly butchered calf that they hadn't touched, they would be looking for the thief with murder on their minds. He wanted them to give up searching for them in confusion after following a dead-end trail.

He wrapped the meat into one of his furs to keep the blood from dripping and began their trip eastward. Sundu led the way with Noonalook following, covering their tracks.

After they had traveled this way for close to two miles, Noonalook redirected their path back to the north once more. The day was late, and he looked for a place to stay overnight. He was confident they hadn't left a trail for someone to find, but once they built a fire that night, their location would be given away in mere moments. He would like to find someplace where they could make a fire to cook their food and not be seen.

Noonalook eventually found a space between three massive boulders. There were no clouds so they wouldn't have to worry about rain and would sleep under the stars again. Noonalook stood in the center of the stones and looked around. He couldn't see over the rocks, and that meant someone on the other side couldn't see them. He dropped his pack, and he and Sundu wandered about looking for firewood.

They gathered an armload of wood, then Noonalook worked to make the fire while Sundu continued to collect more. Noonalook's shoulder wasn't quite as stiff or sore as it had been, but the rhythm of working the stones to make sparks made Noonalook's shoulder ache.

The flames grew and gave off more light revealing something moving near one of the boulders. Noonalook crawled to it and found a small box turtle similar to the ones Sundu had carried before. He smiled and hid it in his pack as a surprise for Sundu.

Sundu returned with an armload of wood, and set it next to Noonalook, and left again to get more. To not draw attention to themselves, Noonalook built a fire up while there was still daylight, getting a good bed of coals. He cut the skin off the calf leg along with some of the extra meat and cooked them separately. Sundu returned once more, dropping the wood in a pile, then sat beside Noonalook to watch and smell the meat cook. Noonalook pulled the turtle out of the bag and gave it to Sundu. Sundu smiled and turned the turtle over, examining it, then looked back up at Noonalook, worry showing on his face.

"Stemma?" asked Sundu, pretending to eat the turtle.

"Hendi," said Noonalook, using Sundu's word.

Noonalook ate a thin slice of the cooked meat then gave some to Sundu. Sundu tried to feed the turtle a tiny piece of meat, but the turtle refused it. Noonalook bit off a small part of one of the apples, and gave it to Sundu, pointing at the turtle. Sundu set the piece of apple before the turtle. The turtle smelled it, then jerked its head forward and ate it. Sundu laughed, and Noonalook gave him another bit of apple for the reptile.

The next day was overcast and colder than it had been the past few days. Noonalook and Sundu tied extra skins over themselves for warmth, but soon, it wouldn't be enough. Sundu shivered as he held the turtle close to his body to keep it warm. Noonalook knew he would have to make boots to keep them from freezing their toes off. He'd known men who had lost their toes, and he had seen toes freeze and turn black then fall off with a horrible smell. A lot of times, those men would die. He had also seen men burn themselves because their feet had become numb with the cold, and they put them too near the fire for too long.

The wind blew in their faces from the north, making it difficult and tiring to walk. It was close to midday, and the sky hadn't gotten any brighter than it had been that morning. The land had flattened out again, and the grasses grew taller. Trees were scarce, and the exposed rocks were now behind them.

On the horizon ahead, were several large brown objects. To Noonalook, they appeared to be shelters. His heart jumped, wondering if he'd finally caught up with the tribe, or was this some other people? As he watched for people, one of the brown things moved. He knew now it was a group of mammoths, and he knew they were dangerous, especially in numbers. They were not as quick-tempered as the rhinoceroses had been, but he didn't want to provoke them.

Noonalook pointed the mammoths out to Sundu and for him to be quiet. The large animals frightened Sundu, and Noonalook smiled to ease the boy's fears. They altered their course, going well around the giant animals, but still passed close enough to see a baby nursing and two juveniles sparring with their growing tusks.

Noonalook watched the mammoths lazily graze on the golden grasses and seemed to not have a care or worry in the world. To Noonalook, they appeared content and happy in their austere lives, surrounded by family and friends. Thinking back, Noonalook had felt that way when he had been with his family and had been chief, even though he worked hard and had a lot of responsibilities. That was the happiest he had ever been in his whole life, and it wasn't long after that he became the most miserable.

While he had been healing after the lion attack, another man rose up and became chief. It came as no surprise to Noonalook, and he had expected it would happen, and he didn't care. Noonalook was useless as chief, so he let the man have it unchallenged.

Every agonizing day he waited and longed to die, but that moment never came. Instead of getting worse and dying, he got better. Looking at his chewed up arm and leg, he wondered what good he would ever be to anyone. He was barely able to take care of himself, how would he ever be able to take care of a family once again? And what women would ever want him now that he was so ugly and helpless?

As time passed in the village, the memories of Noonalook's chiefdom and greatness faded away along with the memories of his family. Children grew up not knowing who Noonalook was or what he had at one time been, and they mimicked and mocked him.

Once they passed around the mammoths, Noonalook and Sundu headed north again. Sundu looked back at the mammoths from time to time until they were no longer in sight. Noonalook thought back to those few days ago when he believed he could never hunt again or ever take care of not only himself but a small boy as well. He wondered what had changed. His arm and leg hadn't gotten any better, and, in fact, since the wolf attack, he was now in worse condition than before. He didn't have the shaman's sacred words or the magic markings on his face or body. Noonalook didn't know what it was, but things were different.

Snow-covered mountains and the familiar crow-head peak lined the horizon under the still overcast sky. A large number of bison and deer grazed on the dried grass as Noonalook and Sundu crossed the vast prairie. The animals were too far away and too fast for Noonalook to hunt unless he found one in his same disfigured condition.

Noonalook found no suitable place to stay the night and hated having to sleep out in the open. Scrub bushes stretched across the land without a single tree nearby, and because of the scarcity of wood, there would be no fire. Looking at the cloud-covered sky, Noonalook couldn't be sure if any rain would come or not, but it would definitely be a cold night.

They rested briefly once more to eat and drink. With no camp to make, no animals to hunt, and no wood for a fire, there was no point in stopping the day's trek early.

They continued on and stopped when it was too dark to see. In the distance looked to be a forest, but it was too far to walk this night. The wind blew harshly across the prairie from the north. Noonalook found a small grouping of scrub bushes and secured a couple of the skins in their limbs to battle the cold gusts. They ate in the dark, and afterward, Noonalook made Sundu a place to sleep and covered him well with furs. Sundu was exhausted and quickly fell asleep. He then lay close to the bushes, keeping his back to the north and covered himself with the remaining skins. The chilling wind blew through the night, and it took a long time before Noonalook fell asleep.

# EIGHT

Noonalook heard the voices as he slept, and dreamed of a strange people speaking a strange language, but it was Sundu's scream that woke him. Noonalook sat up, grabbing for his spear, and found it gone. Men stood over him and Sundu. Noonalook rubbed his eyes to make sure he wasn't still dreaming.

At first, Noonalook thought they had been found by the men they had stolen from, but in the dim light, he could see he was wrong. These weren't men, but they were Neanderthals.

Noonalook had seen these strange people before but knew little about them. He recalled many years ago, when he had been chief, he and a couple of men had been hunting far from home when they heard screams and men fighting. They traced the noise to a camp of Neanderthals, where he and his men watched in hiding as the Neanderthals beat one of their own to death with rocks and sticks, then cut up the body. Some of it was eaten raw, and some of it was cooked. Noonalook had never witnessed cannibalism before, and it made him sick.

Was this what they had in mind for him and Sundu? Noonalook eyed the men standing around them, trying to read their faces.

One of the Neanderthals pointed Noonalook's spear at Noonalook's chest. Noonalook pushes the spearhead away, but the Neanderthal grunted angrily, and shoved it back, cutting into the flesh.

The other four Neanderthals shouted and pointed at the blood running down Noonalook's torso. The one holding the spear took a step back, looking at the others. "Dunn mo bobo?" he asked.

"Nano bunbun adda toe," said one of the Neanderthals, then he grabbed Sundu and jerked him up. Noonalook lunged for the boy, but the sharp point of his own spear pushed him back. Noonalook caught a glimpse of his knife partially sticking out from under the skin he'd slept on. He sat back down and pushed it farther under the hide. He feared that if he used the knife now, he would be impaled on his own spear, leaving Sundu alone with the Neanderthals.

"Junah ta dodun," said one of the Neanderthals to Noonalook while pointing at Sundu.

Noonalook understood they wanted Sundu, but he didn't know why.

The Neanderthal held Sundu firmly as the boy squirmed to break free. Sundu looked at Noonalook, desperate for help, and Noonalook returned a gentle and slight smile. Sundu appeared to comprehend that Noonalook would help, and he stopped fighting. Noonalook was thankful Sundu had become more trusting of him.

Two Neanderthals dragged Sundu away from the campsite. The other three stayed with Noonalook, holding him back with the spear.

"Noonalook!" Sundu cried out. "Noona-!" The boy's plea was muffled by a hand.

Noonalook knew they were keeping him here until the others got away with Sundu, but he wasn't sure why they hadn't killed him yet instead of holding him here. For whatever reason they had, they wanted Sundu alive, and as long as the boy was living, Noonalook would get him back. No matter how far they traveled or difficult the path, he knew he could track them down.

Noonalook looked at the three remaining Neanderthals and smiled at them as he sat on the skins.

"Muno du toma?" asked one of the Neanderthals.
"Gama lo nee do ta?" asked the other.

Seemingly unsure of what to think of Noonalook's unusual behavior, the three Neanderthals looked to one another for answers. Noonalook pretended not to notice the Neanderthals or care that Sundu had been taken away.

"Dundun," said a Neanderthal as he backed away from the others. He squinted out into the night as if trying to find the Neanderthals with Sundu.

"Dundun," he said again to the two Neanderthals. Noonalook noticed he didn't have any teeth.

"Gondon," said the one with Noonalook's spear.

"Tonjo mondoni," said the third, pointing into the dark.

Noonalook watched them from the corner of his eye. The toothless one wanted to leave, and the other two seemed to be staying. He still hadn't figured out if they were going to kill him or not, but when they made their next move, he would be ready for them.

"Dundun," repeated the toothless one.

"Ga-Ga!" said the Neanderthal with the spear. He was angry and waved his hand as if to send away the toothless Neanderthal.

"Dundun," the Neanderthal with no teeth said once more, then left.

"Bahh. Bundo tenona dendy," said the Neanderthal with the spear to the other as they both watched Noonalook.

Noonalook sensed they were uneasy, especially the one holding his spear. The Neanderthal pointed the spear at Noonalook as his jittery feet shuffled in the dirt from one foot to the other, then slowly approached Noonalook.

"Stemma?" asked Noonalook with a smile.

The two Neanderthals watched Noonalook slowly pull two large pieces of leftover bison out of his pack, then offer the meat to them. They snatched the meat from Noonalook's hands. They smelled it, tasted it, and liked it.

Standing, Noonalook stealthily slid the knife into his belt behind his back, using the pack as a cover. The Neanderthals tensed up, but Noonalook smiled as he pulled a smaller piece of bison from the bag and took a bite. The Neanderthals relaxed once again and continued to devour the meat.

Noonalook stood in front of the Neanderthal with the spear, and grinned and nodded at him, but he was busy eating. Noonalook dropped the bag between himself and the Neanderthal, and the Neanderthals looked down at the pack in the dirt as Noonalook reached back and clasped the knife. Noonalook bent down to get the bag, but grabbed the end of the spear instead, and came up quickly, thrusting the blade deep into the Neanderthal's throat. As the Neanderthal staggered about in a panic, Noonalook yanked the spear away from him.

The other Neanderthal rushed to Noonalook, but the old man spun around and shoved the spear into the last Neanderthal. The Neanderthal tried to reach for Noonalook, but the spear held him back until he was too weak to stand.

Noonalook pulled the spear out with a sneer, letting the dead Neanderthal fall, then Noonalook turned back to the other, finding him on the ground with the dagger still in his neck. Noonalook pulled out the knife, with bloody bubbles popping up from the deep wound, and wiped the blade on the dying Neanderthal.

Noonalook quickly crammed his belongings into the pack and throwing it, and the water bladders over his shoulder then ran into the darkness.

He searched through the dark as he ran, trying to find evidence of the Neanderthal's direction of travel, but it was nearly impossible. There was only one word the Neanderthals had used that stuck with Noonalook. He didn't know what the word meant, but it didn't matter; the Neanderthals did, and that was all he needed.

"Dundun," Noonalook called out.

Except for the sounds of the night songs of birds and crickets, there were no other sounds.

"Dundun!" he called louder.

"Doonga?" came a voice from the darkness.

Noonalook determined the direction of the voice, but couldn't see anything.

"Eh?" asked Noonalook.

"Doonga?" The voice was much closer now.

Ahead, a faint figure emerged, waving in the dark.

"Doonga," the Neanderthal said, still waving.

"Ah," said Noonalook, and he ran toward the Neanderthal with his spear ready.

By the time Noonalook was close enough for the Neanderthal to recognize him, it was too late. The last thing the Neanderthal saw was the fierceness in Noonalook's eyes as the old man rammed the spear through him. The Neanderthal's cry was more of a surprise than of pain.

The weight of the spear grew heavier as the Neanderthal's knees weakened. Noonalook pulled the spear out and let the Neanderthal drop.

He stepped away from the body and searched the ground for clues, finding a slight trace of a trail of broken grass stems through the weeds. It was too easy to lose the path in the dark, so he followed slowly and carefully. He glanced up at the stars to orient himself and find the time. He had about two hours to find Sundu before sunrise and escape into the darkness. That would be the ideal plan, but Noonalook knew that ideal hardly ever happened.

Noonalook lost the trail several times as he followed it into a forest, where it was even darker inside. Tracking footprints while nearly blind from the blackness took longer than Noonalook had hoped, and when the light was bright enough to see, he didn't need it anymore. The smells of smoke and cooking food drifting on the wind guided Noonalook better than searching the ground. When he heard the Neanderthals talking, he knew he'd found their camp.

He stepped carefully to avoid the crunchy leaves underfoot, and when he spotted movement ahead, he crouched low and hid behind a tree. Too many trees and undergrowth blocked his view of the campsite, and he crept from the tree to get closer.

He sneaked close enough to the camp to where he could now see a few Neanderthals. Their encampment was made up of several lean-to structures with sticks and skins for roofs. At least twenty Neanderthals were in the camp with several children, and all of them watched something Noonalook couldn't see from his vantage point, so he moved closer.

Noonalook discovered the Neanderthals were watching Sundu. The boy's hands and neck were tied to a tree, which kept him from moving about. There was another boy, close to Sundu's age, lying on the ground. The boy lying down looked strange, but Noonalook couldn't understand why. A male and female stood between the boys, and another man, wearing a mask resembling a bird's face, danced and chanted around the boys. The masked man shook a stick with feathers tied to it at Sundu, and then at the boy on the ground as he half sang his incantations of unintelligible words.

Noonalook found it peculiar that the boy on the ground never moved, no matter how loud the bird-man shouted or how close he danced to the boy. After further observation, Noonalook noticed that the boy's color was wrong, and he looked fat or bloated; either way, he was bigger than the other children in the camp. He then realized the boy was dead and had been for a couple of days by the look of him.

Noonalook watched the feathered stick shake in front of Sundu and then the dead boy. The man moved from one boy to the other, back and forth, while reciting his enchanted words. Sundu, then the boy on the ground; Sundu and back to the dead boy; the living boy, the dead boy. Was the bird-man trying to take the life of Sundu and put it into the dead boy?

Noonalook believed holy men possessed the power to wield the magic, and he believed magic had brought him back from the brink of death. He had seen the sick people of his village healed with magic, but he had never seen the life of the living put into the dead to make them live again. These were strange people. They looked different, and maybe their magic was different, too. If their magic could bring the dead back to life, what would happen to Sundu? Would he die? Noonalook would not let that happen. He didn't come all this way to let Sundu's life be given to some unfortunate boy.

Noonalook needed to get Sundu out of there before the magic could take effect. Sundu still looked healthy and very much alive, but Noonalook didn't know for how much longer.

He quickly backed into the cover of the thick forest. They would both end up dead if he took the risk of going through the middle of the campsite to rescue Sundu. He would have to be sneaky about it and fast. He ran quietly through the forest, around the campsite, and ended up some distance behind Sundu.

Everyone watched the holy man, waiting for the miracle to happen, and Noonalook had to be careful getting closer to Sundu. With all of those eyes pointed in his direction, it wouldn't take much movement to catch someone's eye.

He crept on his belly closer to the edge of the camp and hid behind another tree. He paused for a moment to catch his breath and formulate a plan, but there was no time for intricate strategies, he just needed to get Sundu and get away as quickly as possible without getting killed.

He took off the pack and water bladders and set them on the ground. He needed to be as nimble as possible, and everything but his spear and knife would be a hindrance. He would grab his things on the way out with Sundu.

He pulled himself along the ground toward the tree Sundu was tied to, dragging the spear with him. He kept his eyes on the Neanderthal's eyes, scanning from one to the other, to make sure no one had caught sight of him yet.

Before he reached the tree, one of the females spotted him. At first, she did nothing but watch him, but when she realized Noonalook wasn't an animal or one of her people, she shrieked and pointed at him.

Noonalook jumped to his feet, raised his spear and charged at the Neanderthals, yelling his war cry. The Neanderthals darted backward and scattered, scrambling to scrounge up whatever weapons they could find. Sundu had been crying the entire time he had been tied to the tree but laughed out loud when Noonalook appeared.

Noonalook passed Sundu and ran straight for the shaman, who was just as stunned as everyone else and impaled him on the spear. The holy man's death meant life for Sundu. Noonalook extracted the spear from the dying man's body and used it to cut Sundu's bindings.

"Noonalook!" Sundu said, wiping his tears and hugging Noonalook.

Noonalook smiled, then pushed him toward the forest. "Bardoni! Bardoni!" he shouted.

When Sundu saw the men coming after them with clubs and spears, he screamed and ran with Noonalook following. They ran through the underbrush and around the trees. Sundu ran faster and gained distance on Noonalook. They passed the tree where Noonalook left the pack and water bladders, but there wasn't a second to spare to grab them, and they were left behind. Without that pack, there would be no skins, no fire, and no food. Their journey would be more strenuous without the bag, but there would be no journey at all if he didn't have Sundu, or if they didn't get away from the Neanderthals.

Sundu looked back to see Noonalook lagging behind, and he stopped to wait.

Noonalook shook his head and motioned for Sundu to keep running.

"Bardoni! Bardoni!" he shouted short of breath, and Sundu turned and ran on into the forest.

Noonalook's legs ached, and his lungs burned. He knew if he stopped to fight, he would not survive. He also knew he couldn't outrun them. They were far younger than he was, and they didn't have the mangled muscles he had.

Sundu ran farther and faster ahead as Noonalook uncontrollably slowed down. His hip joints felt as if bone ground against bone from sprinting and at such an odd position, compensating for his missing leg muscles.

Noonalook didn't think he could keep going much longer. Sundu had a good chance he'd escaped and had run so far ahead that Noonalook couldn't see him anymore. He wished he'd given Sundu the knife so at least he could defend himself should the Neanderthals eventually catch up with him.

A spear whizzed by Noonalook, barely missing him and stuck into the ground in front of him. He jumped over the spear and kept running, wondering if the next spear would get him in the back.

Noonalook couldn't get enough air and felt like passing out. He tried to push his body to keep going, but his legs gave out, and he stumbled to the ground.

He quickly rolled over and pointed his spear at the Neanderthals, stopping them. There were six males, and they varied in age from old to young. Sweat ran into Noonalook's eyes and mouth as he breathed heavily, and fought the sensation of blacking out. He jabbed his spear at them and growled like an animal to keep them back as he slowly got back to his feet.

The Neanderthals looked at one another then back to Noonalook as he stepped forward and threatened them with the spear again. A few of the Neanderthals took a step backward.

"Noonalook!" Sundu called from somewhere in the forest.

"Bardoni!" Noonalook yelled back in a hoarse voice between deep breaths.

Noonalook scrutinized the Neanderthals, watching for any slight movement.

"Noonalook!" came Sundu's voice again, this time sounding desperate.

"Bardoni!" repeated Noonalook.

"Hendi!"

Something was wrong, and Noonalook knew Sundu, for whatever reason, could not go any farther. The Neanderthals looked beyond Noonalook into the woods, searching for the boy.

Noonalook didn't know if he had the strength to run again. The men before him seemed barely out of breath at all. He took a small step backward as he thrust the spear at them repeatedly. Noonalook took two more steps backward, and the Neanderthals didn't move, except for one, and he looked as if he wanted to challenge Noonalook. The man was young, eager, and angry. Noonalook determined if he wasn't the chief already, he one day would be. If any of these men were to attack first, Noonalook knew it would be this one.

Noonalook stepped back two more steps, and the young Neanderthal smiled and stepped forward. The other men, with newfound courage, stepped forward also. Noonalook growled again, and poked the spear at them, knowing his threats were wearing thin, and at any second, they could rush and overtake him.

Noonalook couldn't take the chance of an attack, and jumped forward, yelling and swinging his spear before all of them. The Neanderthals readied their weapons, but also backed up to avoid the spear, except, again, the young one.

The man wanted the fight. Noonalook knew

he looked like an easy win to the young man, and why wouldn't he? He was going up against someone more than twice his age and could hardly use his arm and leg, but age and scars develop experience, and that's what Noonalook relied on. The ways of war had become an instinct.

"Naungaw!" said Noonalook as he stared the young man in the eye.

He took a step back, then another. Adjusting the spear in his hand, the young Neanderthal took a step forward, leaving the others behind.

Noonalook ran to the young Neanderthal, shouting his war cry. The Neanderthal, full of aggression and confidence, held up his own spear, and stepped forward, anxious to kill the old man.

Noonalook stretched out his spear as far as he could. The two spears collided, and Noonalook ran his spearhead down the shank of the young man's spear, cutting the hands of the Neanderthal. The young man jerked his hands back, dropping the spear, and leaving no defense. Noonalook plunged the spear deep into the young Neanderthal's chest, breaking through ribs, and it all had taken place in a flash. There was fury in the Neanderthal's face as he grabbed Noonalook's spear with both hands.

The other Neanderthals stepped back in disbelief. Noonalook tried to pull his spear from the Neanderthal's chest, but the young man would not let go and seemed to pull it farther inside himself. Noonalook knew he wasn't getting the spear back and pushed it with all of his strength, sending the young Neanderthal stumbling backward till he fell. The other Neanderthals watched the young man lay on the ground with the spear sticking straight up. Blood seeped from the chest wound and trickled out of the Neanderthal's mouth as he died.

Noonalook whirled around and bolted. He didn't have to look back to know if he was being chased, the Neanderthals' own war cries rang in his ears as they tore through the forest after him.

"Sundu!" Noonalook called out.

"Noonalook!" Sundu replied somewhere far ahead.

Noonalook pulled out his knife, and a kind of comfort coursed through him as he held it tightly in his grasp. He hoped it would be enough to get him and Sundu out of this mess.

"Noonalook!" came Sundu's voice again, giving Noonalook a direction to follow.

As Noonalook approached Sundu, an unfamiliar sound, like the continuous roar of a strong wind, increased in intensity as he drew closer. He finally spotted Sundu jumping up and down and waving his arms in a small clearing with bright sunlight shining on him. The angry Neanderthals behind were closing in on Noonalook fast, shouting and shaking their spears and clubs.

Sundu yelled something and pointed down. When Noonalook finally reached Sundu, he discovered both what the sound was and what had kept Sundu from moving on. Beyond them was a forty-foot deep chasm carved by a rushing river.

"Duntoo," said Noonalook under his breath.

He had never seen a river such as this. They couldn't swim in water like this, but they couldn't keep running, either. The Neanderthals were only seconds away from capturing them. Noonalook secured the knife in his belt, grabbed Sundu, and jumped into the icy water. The Neanderthals stopped at the edge of the cliff, shouting and waving their weapons.

By the time Noonalook and Sundu resurfaced, they had already been swept far along the river in the swift current. Noonalook looked back to find their pursuers far behind, running along the edge of the chasm, silhouetted against the bright morning sky, still chasing them. Noonalook pulled Sundu close where the boy wrapped his arms around Noonalook's neck and tightly held on as he fought to keep his head above the water.

Noonalook tried to swim to the riverbank, but the current pulled him back to the center. The river's mighty torrent was too strong for Noonalook to stop when he tried digging his feet into the river bottom. He fought to hang on to the large rocks sticking up out of the water as they passed by, but they were too slick with slimy moss, and they floated downstream with the flow.

Behind them, the Neanderthals still ran along the edge of the chasm, but they had dropped very far back now. Noonalook felt they had escaped, but it would be in his and Sundu's advantage to stay with the swift current for a while longer to get as far as possible from the Neanderthals.

Exhaustion crept into Noonalook's body as the weight of Sundu made it harder to stay afloat, and the freezing water sucked the warmth and energy from him. They needed to get out of the water to the north side of the river.

After several minutes, the Neanderthals couldn't be seen anymore, and Noonalook began looking for a way out of the water. It wasn't long before he spotted a dead tree lying in the river with the back half on land on the north side.

"Sundu, stedona mellekon," Noonalook said as he pointed to the log.

Sundu nodded, seeming to understand the log could help them out of the river. Noonalook reasoned if he could at least get Sundu out of the water, then he would have a better chance at getting himself out. The swiftness of the current drove them closer to the log. Noonalook tried to push the boy away from him, but Sundu wouldn't let go.

"Sundu, gello nar nodum," Noonalook said and pointed at the log. "Stedona mellekon."

Noonalook knew Sundu was scared, and maybe he didn't understand what he had said. Noonalook tried to swim toward the log, fighting the current pulling them back to the middle. He stretched out and grabbed the edge of it with one hand. The tree shifted with their weight, and Noonalook lost his grip. He reached out with his other hand and caught it once again, but the force knocked Sundu loose, and he drifted away. Noonalook lurched and snagged Sundu's arm while still holding the log with his other hand, straining to hold onto both.

"Sundu, stedona mellekon," Noonalook said wearily through clenched teeth as he pulled Sundu back to himself.

Sundu grabbed the log and pulled himself to the riverbank. Once Sundu was safely on the shore, Noonalook dragged himself along the tree, finally crawling out of the water and lay on the rocks.

He then remembered the strange people chasing them, and looked about, but didn't see anyone. He motioned for Sundu to follow, and they climbed up the steep embankment, entering into the thicket of trees growing along the river, and walked far enough into the woods to not be seen from the water.

Noonalook sat and leaned against a tree. He was drained and had to rest before they moved on. He had no idea how far they'd been swept down the river or where they were, and he wasn't sure if Sundu's tribe had crossed the river or had even made it this far. They could be anywhere by now, and it was too overwhelming to think about how he'd ever find them.

He looked at Sundu sitting close by, watching him and shivering. Noonalook wished there could be something he could do for him, but at the moment, there was nothing. He smiled at Sundu and patted his leg, then closed his eyes.

Noonalook woke with a start, thinking the Neanderthals had found them. He looked around, seeing only Sundu playing with sticks. Sundu saw Noonalook was awake and smiled at him. Noonalook returned an assuring smile and nodded, wanting Sundu to know everything was all right.

Noonalook stood with the aid of the tree and stretched his sore muscles. From the way the light shone through the trees, he could tell he'd slept a couple of hours. He was cold and hungry and knew the boy must feel the same way.

He slowly walked back toward the river, scanning for any signs of the Neanderthals. Sundu walked beside him, and together, they crept to the edge of the woods. With no water bladders, they needed to drink before leaving the river, and

Noonalook wanted to find more flint rocks for a fire-making kit and more tools.

They waited in the outskirts of the forest and watched the opposite side of the river but saw nothing.

The singing birds and the chattering squirrels gave Noonalook a peace of mind that no one had been around recently. He wondered if the Neanderthals had given up on them or maybe thought they had drowned in the river.

Noonalook made his way down the rocky bank with Sundu. They walked to the water and drank, then Noonalook searched along the edge of the river looking at the stones. He pushed them around with his feet, picking some up for closer examination, and eventually found three useful flint rocks.

He looked around to get his bearings. Only parts of the mountains were visible in the west, from where the river flowed, but trees obscured the northern mountains to which they had been walking. If they followed the river back upstream, it meant having a constant water supply. Still, it also meant passing the Neanderthals again, but least the river separated them from one another. Noonalook then wondered how many other tribes had made their camps or villages near the water.

Noonalook and Sundu climbed back up the bank and disappeared in the woods. He kept his eyes on the river below, looking for Neanderthals.

About an hour later, Noonalook stopped and held out his hand for Sundu to stop, then pointed across the river. Sundu took a few steps back to hide behind Noonalook when he saw two female

Neanderthals drinking at the river's edge. Noonalook and Sundu carefully stepped farther back into the thick of the forest and continued their journey. The roar of the river was loud enough to cover their footsteps, but quick movements could possibly be seen.

Noonalook and Sundu crouched low as they passed the Neanderthals. When they had gone far enough away that the women couldn't be seen anymore, they straightened and walked at a faster pace.

Sundu pulled the fur Noonalook wore. He stopped and looked about for danger, but didn't see anything, then looked down at Sundu, who pointed to the ground. They stood amid hundreds of fallen pecans. Noonalook had been so concerned with the river and the other possible people living near it that he had not been looking for anything else.

He picked up a couple and broke them open only to find them rotten, but he found fresh pecans still in the tree. He picked off what he could reach and shared them with Sundu. They hadn't eaten since the night before, and both were hungry. When he had picked all he could reach, Noonalook lifted Sundu, placing him on his shoulders. Sundu laughed, but Noonalook gestured for him to be quiet. Noonalook walked about under the tree with Sundu softly giggling as he stretched up to pick more pecans.

After stripping the tree of nuts, and eating them, they continued on. Both were thirsty from the pecans, but Noonalook wanted to wait until they were much farther from the Neanderthals before he dared go to the river again.

An hour later, Noonalook led Sundu down to

the river where they drank. The current was still swift, but the lack of large rocks in the water kept it from roaring. The mountains couldn't be seen for all of the trees, but once they left this forest, and got back out to the plains, he would look for the crow-head peak. If they happened upon another trail, Noonalook would not follow it. There was hardly a chance it would be Sundu's tribe, and a path out here could only lead to more trouble.

Sundu screamed behind Noonalook, making the old man jump. He whirled around and whipped out his knife to find Sundu, pointing at a long, black snake. All Noonalook knew about snakes was if you got bit by one, sometimes you got sick or died, like his father, and sometimes you didn't. He       didn't know if this was the dangerous kind or not, but he knew he could eat it.

He grabbed the snake by its tail, swung it up in the air, and back down, smashing its head against a rock. He dropped the snake and let it coil and thrash around until it died. They wouldn't be able to eat it until they could get far enough away to build a fire to cook it.

They left the river and headed north through the forest.

They traveled the rest of the day through the woods, and just before sundown, Noonalook finally saw the end of the forest.

When it was dark, they stopped to sleep. The north wind blew gently but cold. Noonalook had Sundu lay down, and he covered the boy with dead leaves. It wouldn't be much to battle the cold, but it would help a little, and help keep them hidden from any passersby. He then lay down close by, putting the dead snake next to him to keep it from getting stolen in the night, and covered himself with leaves.

The birds in the forest began their songs as hints of the rising sun appeared through the trees. Noonalook woke cold, stiff, sore, and itchy. He rose slightly, checking his surroundings to make sure no one had found them. He sat up, letting the leaves fall and scratched his arm and side. He looked to see what made him itch and found ants crawling on him. He knocked them off and scratched himself. Sundu's leaf pile was undisturbed, and beyond Sundu, fragments of the mountains, with their snowy peaks, and orange from the morning light, shown through the gaps between trees.

He watched two squirrels chase one another up and down a tree as he tried to wake up, then painfully stood to his feet. The dead snake was still beside him, and he picked it up. Ants crawled all over it and onto his hand. Now he knew where the ants had come from. He dropped the snake and shook off the ants and scratched again.

Sundu stirred from all of the noise Noonalook had made and sat up. Sundu shivered in the morning temperatures, and Noonalook knew the only way they could get warm was to start walking. He helped Sundu to his feet, then picked up the snake. He brushed off the remaining ants, and draped it over his shoulder, then started for the mountains with Sundu trailing behind sleepily.

As they walked across the prairie-like grasslands, the north wind blew against them, and the long grass was wet with dew, chilling them. The mountain range stretched across the horizon, but the crow-head peak was nowhere to be seen. Perhaps the crow-head peak's appearance had been altered since their location had changed so drastically. Noonalook knew these were the correct mountains, but as he and Sundu drew closer to them, they had become unrecognizable.

The cold wind reminded him he would now have to focus on surviving the winter and hope to find a cave with a water source and game to hunt nearby. He wasn't sure how Sundu would take never seeing his mother again if she was even still alive, or his tribe. Maybe the boy already suspected that he would never see them again, but didn't know how to express it. He and Sundu would have to learn each other's language, and there would be plenty of time for that during the winter.

The mountains before them should have many caves in them, and there looked to be plenty of trees in the vicinity, and Noonalook was sure he could find water nearby also. He studied the mountains and wondered where he should go. Which area would be best for them? From this distance, he couldn't see much detail of the mountains, only snow on the top and dark, rocky regions below. There were many hills to cross before they reached the mountains, and some of the hills were nearly mountains themselves.

Noonalook gave Sundu one of the rocks from the river to hold, and he set about banging the two remaining stones together, shaping one with the other. Creating stone tools was the one thing Noonalook had been good at before and since the lion attack. He needed to make spearheads and extra knives, but he wanted to make something special first. He chipped away at it for hours as they walked, skillfully shaping the rock. Ahead was a group of trees, and he decided to stop there and cook the snake before it decayed.

By the time they reached the group of trees, Noonalook had finished his flint rock project. He had chiseled out a little knife similar to his own but made for a smaller hand. He turned to Sundu with the present hidden behind his back and took back the rough flint rock Sundu had carried. Noonalook held out the knife for Sundu and watched as the boy's face brightened when he saw it. Sundu looked up at Noonalook, who grinned and placed the gift in the boy's hand. Sundu turned it over and over, examining every inch of it, then held it in his hand as if to stab, and practiced in the air.

Noonalook left Sundu to play with the new knife as he gathered and stacked firewood in a pile. After collecting a handful of tinder, Noonalook balled it up and placed it between two thick sticks. He took the two remaining flintstones and struck them together. It took a while before he finally produced a spark, but once a few sparks landed in the tinder, it began to smolder.

Noonalook kept the fire small for fear of a visit from another unfriendly tribe, but the small fire meant the snake took longer to cook. After they ate, Noonalook covered the burned wood with dirt and rocks to hide it.

They left the little grove of trees and headed toward the mountains. The land was not as flat as it had been, and they would soon be getting into the hills leading to the mountains. Noonalook wasn't sure how he would fare over this new terrain but knew he would slow their trip down even more.

They found a small stream and made their camp there for the night. Their lack of firewood kept their fire small and short-lived. Their dinner consisted of crawfish and frogs, which they caught in the stream. There were no leaves to cover with that night, and they slept out in the open, close to the glowing coals.

Noonalook woke later in the night with Sundu curled up at his back, trying to keep warm. He had a hard time going back to sleep as he worried about all the things he had to do to survive the winter. He would have to hunt many animals to provide enough skins for him and the boy, and at the same time, find enough food to keep them both from starving to death.

He thought back to how simple his life had been when he'd lived alone in his little home, scrounging for food and firewood, but his life had also been a lot emptier. Noonalook wasn't sure how, but Sundu had brought out the good man he used to be, and the confidence he had lost long ago. He wondered what would happen to himself if Sundu ever did return to his tribe. Would he go back to his shelter on the outskirts of the village to be teased and made fun of again? Would he go back to eating bugs and hating himself? Could he really ever live like that again? Sundu had awoken emotions and strengths in him that he hadn't felt in years, and he knew he would miss the boy once he was gone. Noonalook felt melancholic as he looked up at the stars, wishing the feeling would go away, but it held on to him until he fell asleep.

# NINE

The cold made it too difficult to sleep, so Noonalook and Sundu started out early the next morning. They drank as much as they could from the stream before leaving. The morning light revealed the grassy hills and valleys stretching for miles, gradually gaining in height and depth the closer they were to the mountains.

As Noonalook and Sundu descended into a valley, Sundu caught sight of something big, cutting through the tall grass. He cried out and grabbed Noonalook. Noonalook turned to look where Sundu pointed but saw nothing. He waited only a moment later before giving up and moving on.

Sundu stayed close to Noonalook, his eyes continually darting back and around. Every time the wind blew the grass, Sundu jumped, making Noonalook nervous. He didn't know what Sundu had seen, but it had to have been something more than just the wind. Rabbits had been scurrying through the weeds, and Noonalook thought maybe one had jumped nearby and scared him.

They reached the bottom of the valley and began to cross it when something at the top of the hill to his right caught Noonalook's eye, but when he looked, it was gone. He didn't know what it was, but it had to be fast because it had disappeared before he could see it. Was this the same thing the boy had seen?

Sundu screamed. Noonalook caught the movement from his left side this time. A cave lion emerged from the grass near them. Noonalook stumbled backward, tripping over Sundu, and both fell. Noonalook pulled out his knife and held it before him.

"Bembama lo manda, Sundu!" said Noonalook, short of breath and heart pounding.

Noonalook stood with shaky knees, placing himself in front of Sundu, and kept his eyes on Shokona. The cave lion only watched them, and sniffed the air, catching their scents on the breeze. Could this really be Shokona? The scars he had put on the great cat told Noonalook it was Shokona, but how and why had Shokona followed them?

Noonalook couldn't read any ferociousness in Shokona's eyes, nor could he find any anger or cruelty, and the cat didn't appear to be preparing for an attack. This was the first time Noonalook had seen the lion in the daytime for years and noticed Shokona's muzzle was gray, and his scared skin hung loosely from his bones. Noonalook had never thought of Shokona's age before and wondered how long cave lions lived. Shokona looked old and tired and lonely.

Noonalook thought back to the few times he

had seen Shokona and remembered the cat was always alone. Had Shokona been exiled from his people just as he had been?

Noonalook's mind raced with questions, but how could anyone understand the thoughts and actions of an animal? Why did Shokona show himself now? And during the day? Shokona could have easily attacked him and Sundu in their sleep last night, or even right now. Could the cat remember Noonalook's scent after all of these years? He and Shokona shared permanent injuries and scars from that day. Did Shokona remember the battle they had in which no one won?

How many times had Noonalook left his village and sought out the lion? Called his name? How many years had he waited for Shokona to finish the job he had started so long ago? Day after day, in pain and in heartache, he awaited to die. Why did Shokona show himself now? This was not the time to die. If he could make Shokona understand that once Sundu had a safe place to live, he would come back and let the lion end it all.

The lion slowly stalked around Noonalook and Sundu in a broad circle, growling softly. Shokona limped when he walked, and his muscles looked stiff. He stopped and stared at Noonalook, and the old man sensed that something was going to happen.

Noonalook looked back at Sundu and saw the boy was terrified. He hugged Sundu, then turned him to face the mountains. The boy had a better chance on his own than he did staying and fighting Shokona, and if he kept walking, there was the chance that he would find a tribe to take care of him.

"Sundu, bardoni," Noonalook said as he

pushed Sundu away and pointed to the mountains.

"Hendi!" cried Sundu.

Sundu quickly turned and grabbed onto the old man, hugging him tightly. Noonalook smiled and patted the boy gently on the back. He pulled himself away from Sundu and wiped the tears from the boy's cheek.

Noonalook pointed his knife at Shokona for Sundu to see. If Shokona wanted a battle, then Noonalook would provide one, but he couldn't let the lion win now. Noonalook was forced to fight for Sundu's life. Noonalook knew that if he couldn't win against Shokona, then he would have to at least injure the lion enough to keep him from harming Sundu. Noonalook would fight Shokona with the very knife he had used those many years ago. Tooth and claw against knife. Shokona would remember the blade's piercing pain once again.

Noonalook turned Sundu back to the mountains and gave him a slight push. After a few steps forward, Sundu stopped and looked back at Noonalook. The old man stood as straight and as tall as he could with his chest out. He tapped the knife against his chest and pointed it back to Shokona. Then he pointed with his other hand down to Sundu then up to the mountains beyond.

"Sundu, bardoni," Noonalook repeated.

The boy turned and ran up the hill toward the mountains.

Noonalook turned back to Shokona. This was the day he had waited for, and one way or another, it would finally be over. Even though the day was cold, Noonalook found his palms sweaty, and he readjusted the knife in his hand for a better grip. He took a deep breath, then walked toward Shokona.

He looked for hints of an attack in Shokona's eyes and for any type of movement or tensing muscles, but saw none. Noonalook's heart beat rapidly in anticipation, but he could show no fear. He slowed as he stepped closer to the lion.

Noonalook stopped when Shokona casually looked away and licked his chops, then sat down. Noonalook was confused. Was the animal tricking him? He took a step closer, but the lion seemed to pay no attention to him and only glanced briefly at him. This was not how Shokona was supposed to act. It was as if Shokona had forgotten who he was.

Noonalook edged closer and stopped about eight feet from the lion, and the lion lay down. Noonalook sprang back, thinking the lion would do something, but he stayed on the ground and flicked his tail.

"Shokona!" screamed Noonalook.

The lion raised his head and looked at the old man briefly then rested his head back on the ground.

Noonalook ran at the lion aggressively, holding up the knife, and yelled again.

"Shokona! Wandalla!"

But Shokona didn't move, didn't even flinch, and Noonalook stopped a few feet away from him. He watched the lion for a moment, then looked back at Sundu, who had paused to watch and looked just as confused as Noonalook.

The old man stepped carefully to Shokona until he stood next to the lion, over his bony rib cage. The lion was massive, and in his prime, had been even more prominent with his muscles and more frightening. Noonalook could tell the lion had lost a lot of weight. Maybe Shokona was sick. Noonalook pushed one of the lion's enormous paws with his foot, but the lion only looked at Noonalook, then lay his head back down.

"Shokona?" asked Noonalook.

He walked around to the animal's head, and they met each other's eyes. What was Shokona doing? Noonalook didn't have time to play the animal's game. If Shokona didn't want to fight, then he would leave the animal where it lay and be on his way. Noonalook turned away from the lion and walked back to meet Sundu.

"Noonalook!" cried Sundu, pointing at the lion.

Noonalook spun around to see the lion charging him. Noonalook didn't have time to react and cringed. Shokona brushed the side of his leg as he ran past, knocking the old man down, then stopped and turned back. Noonalook got up, and he and Shokona stood before one another. The lion roared with as much ferocity as it had in its youth, sending chills up Noonalook's spine.

Noonalook brought the knife back up and waited for the attack with clenched teeth, but it never came. Shokona panted with his mouth open and sat back down. Noonalook hesitated for a moment, then lowered the knife, and took a few steps toward the lion. Shokona's heavy panting filled the nearby air with his breath. It smelled rotten. Noonalook stepped closer until they were nearly eye to eye, and he noticed that most of the lion's teeth were missing or broken off. Was this was why he had only eaten the soft parts of the wolves?

Noonalook trembled, unable to distinguish it

from fear or anger. He raised his left hand before Shokona and received no reaction, then he reached up and touched Shokona on the head, keeping the knife clenched tightly in his right. The lion stopped panting and nudged his head against Noonalook's palm. Noonalook jerked his hand away, but when he realized the lion intended no harm, he put his hand back on Shokona's head and rubbed it, feeling ticks beneath the fur.

Could an animal feel regret? Had Shokona come seeking forgiveness? Noonalook didn't know, but he could think of no other reason for the animal's odd behavior. Noonalook couldn't help but smile as he scratched behind the lion's ears. Perhaps a truce had been met. Shokona seemed to show him forgiveness, and Noonalook wanted to return forgiveness to Shokona. He had always dreamed of the day he would either kill or be killed by this animal that had ruined his life. He never thought he would be petting the beast as it purred like a kitten. It didn't seem right, and he backed away.

As quick as lightning, Shokona stretched forward and caught Noonalook's arm in his mouth. Noonalook panicked and tried to pull away, but the lion had him tight. He raised the knife to threaten, but the lion ignored it. Shokona had felt the knife's bite before and was unlikely to forget its sting. Shokona was gentle now, but the broken teeth were jagged and dug into Noonalook's skin. Noonalook lowered his knife, wondering what the lion was doing.

The warmth of the lion's tongue and breath on his arm brought back the terrible memories, reminding Noonalook that this arm had been in the lion's mouth before, but had been subject to a much different experience long ago. The bite had been ferocious and deadly, tearing flesh and breaking bone. The slobber that now dripped from Shokona's mouth had once been Noonalook's blood. His left arm had defended his life as he had desperately stabbed the great cat.

Noonalook looked at the scars cutting through the lion's fur and the scars running up his nearly useless left arm, then to Shokona's eyes where he found sadness. Did Shokona remember that terrible day? Was he trying to recreate it?

Noonalook tried to pull his arm away, but Shokona would not release it. The more Noonalook pulled, the tighter the bite became. Was this another one of Shokona's games? He pulled harder, and Shokona growled. Noonalook cursed himself for being foolish enough to trust Shokona. He then caught sight of Sundu walking back to him with his little knife ready to use. Noonalook waved him back with his free hand.

"Sundu, bardoni!" he shouted.

The loud voice scared Shokona, and he bit harder, hurting Noonalook. The bite broke the skin. Noonalook winced and moaned from the pain. His knees went weak, and he could hardly stand.

"Shokona," he pleaded softly.

He could free himself if he killed Shokona, but something had happened in the past few minutes, and he no longer wanted to kill the lion.

Had he expected more from the lion? Had he mistakenly put people's emotions and thoughts inside this animal? Was Shokona just acting like a cave lion? Was he trying to say something to Noonalook? Noonalook frantically tried to think of possible answers. Had someone in Noonalook's tribe hurt Shokona's family? Killed them? Had it been him? Noonalook had killed many cave lions with his hunting party. He had cut them up and eaten them. He had worn their skins.

"Shokona!" he said as he shook the knife before the lion.

Noonalook knew where the lion's heart was, and he knew he could kill Shokona with one puncture of his blade.

He put the knifepoint against Shokona's rib cage, over the heart, and pushed hard enough to break through the fur and skin. There was no acknowledgment of the blade at all, but there should have been something. Surely Shokona felt the pierce.

Noonalook pushed the knife deeper, and the lion actually loosened his bite but reacted no other way. Noonalook studied Shokona's eyes and found them strangely indifferent to the blade in his rib cage.

Did Shokona want to die?

Noonalook carefully put more pressure on the knife. No reaction.

Shokona wanted to die.

The old man pushed the blade in farther until he felt the beating heart against it. Shokona's panting became erratic and strained. With one forceful shove, Noonalook pushed the knife into Shokona's heart. Shokona released Noonalook's arm and fell to the ground.

Noonalook dropped to his knees and petted the dying lion.

"Shokona?" asked Noonalook.

Shokona looked at him. His panting now gurgled, and blood seeped from his mouth. Shokona then closed his eyes and died.

Sundu ran up Noonalook and looked from the dead cave lion to Noonalook.

Noonalook felt a great sadness, and he cried. He didn't know why he felt this way. The death of Shokona was what he had wanted for so long, but he never imagined it would end like this. Maybe he felt sorrow because Shokona had been a horrible part of his history, and had served as the last link back to his family. Noonalook felt as if his entire life was disintegrating around him like sand in his hand. Everything he was and everyone he knew was gone, and now his past was gone. All he had left was his knife, some fading memories, and this boy to take care of.

Noonalook pulled the knife from the lion and put it back in his belt. He wiped his eyes and put his arm around Sundu's shoulder and continued their journey to the mountains.

Noonalook thought a lot about Shokona as they walked. He and the lion shared a past filled with tragedy and scars, then old age. They shared heartbreak and hatred. And they shared a motive. All this time, Noonalook had wanted Shokona to kill him so he could once again be with his family, but it turned out Shokona had wanted the same thing.

# TEN

Noonalook and Sundu walked for two more days up and down the hills. Both nights they had made fires with the abundance of the scattered trees along the way, and they found small streams to drink from and catch a few small fish and frogs. The temperature had dropped considerably as they moved closer to the mountains, and the wind blew the tall grass like waves across the land.

The mountains towered before them, and they were close enough now to see the details of them and their grandness. They progressed slowly but steadily across the hills, each one higher than the one before it. Large rocks jutted from the ground, and Noonalook searched amongst them for a cave to stay in through the winter. He found a few, but they were either too shallow or too small to live in. Occasionally, Noonalook thought he could see darkened areas in the mountains and foothills and hoped they could be caves since he had found nothing in the hills.

Herds of bison and deer ran across the hills, and the flatlands behind them, and Noonalook knew this would be a good land if they could only find a place to live. He didn't think he was fast enough or limber enough to hunt large, swift animals. In a few years, though, Sundu would be quick and strong enough to kill anything, and Noonalook could teach the boy everything he knew about hunting.

A patch of trees grew on the hill before them. It was getting late, and they would stay there for the night.

As they climbed the last stretch of the hill, a rabbit leaped out of the high grass, scaring Noonalook and Sundu. The frightened rabbit, trying to get away, ran headfirst into a tree, stunning itself for a moment. Noonalook laughed first, then saw an opportunity. Pulling out his knife, Noonalook ran to the rabbit and stabbed it before it could come to its senses and run away. Sundu ran to see the dead rabbit as Noonalook drew the blade from it. Noonalook looked up at Sundu, then put up two fingers like rabbit's ears, made his hand hop about, and hit the tree.

"Bah!" said Noonalook and laid his hand over like the rabbit.

It took a moment for Sundu to understand what game Noonalook played, then he smiled and laughed. Noonalook picked up the rabbit, and Sundu followed him to the top of the hill. Noonalook smiled to himself because not only did they have meat for the night, but now he had a start on collecting fur for winter.

Noonalook dropped the rabbit near a tree at the top of the hill and placed the two flint rocks near it. He pointed at some sticks on the ground near Sundu. Sundu nodded and began picking up firewood.

Noonalook walked through the trees, looking for a place to build a shelter to keep them out of the bitter, cold winds blowing down from the snowy mountain tops. He picked up some of the thicker and longer fallen branches and leaned one end of them upon a low branch, and pushed them into the ground. He didn't have his cord anymore, and the shelter wouldn't be sturdy, but it only had to last one night.

"Sundu," Noonalook called out.

Sundu looked up with his arms full of sticks and saw Noonalook pointing at the crude shelter. Sundu smiled and dropped the wood near the lean-to. Noonalook retrieved the rabbit and flint rocks, then sat down in front of their shelter.

"Sundu," repeated Noonalook, motioning for the boy to sit near him.

Sundu sat down as Noonalook prepared the sticks and kindling for a fire. When he had set it up just right, he handed Sundu the two flintstones and pointed at the wood. Sundu looked concerned at first, but Noonalook smiled, patted the boy on the shoulder, and pointed again at the firewood.

Sundu banged the rocks together, but Noonalook corrected him through demonstration, then handed the stones back to Sundu. With his new knowledge, Sundu struck the stones together over and over but never produced a spark. He looked up to Noonalook in frustration, but the old man just smiled and nodded, and it was enough for Sundu to try again.

It wasn't long before his effort paid off with a

single spark, and it gave Sundu the encouragement to keep working. He continued to make more sparks until one of them ignited the kindling. Sundu smiled, but Noonalook directed him to continue working with the fire. Sundu imitated the way Noonalook blew on the smoldering grass, and a flame sprang to life. Sundu quickly added twigs and tiny sticks to keep it going. Noonalook smiled and patted Sundu on the back, then began preparing the rabbit.

Sundu watched as Noonalook worked with the rabbit, first skinning it, then fastening the rabbit's carcass over the coals to cook. Once the rabbit was roasting, Noonalook propped the skin on sticks next to the fire to help it cure.

Sundu then left to get more wood, and Noonalook returned to work on the shelter, covering it with more long branches. He found a few rocks and put them at the base of the sticks to give it more stability.

When he had finished, he looked it over. There were still gaps in it, and if he had his skins, he could have covered those gaps. Still, it was better than what they'd had the past few nights.

The sun had slowly set behind the mountains, bringing an early sunset and colder winds as the sky darkened. Noonalook found himself humming as he poked at the rabbit and turned it over to cook the other side. Sundu occasionally added more wood to the fire, and Noonalook could tell the boy was proud of what he had done. Noonalook was also proud of Sundu and knew the boy had been paying attention to the skills he had tried to teach.

After the rabbit had cooked, Noonalook removed it from the fire and set it in the grass. He tore off one of the rabbit's hind legs, gave it to Sundu, then pulled off a piece for himself. When Sundu had finished, Noonalook gave him the other back leg. Noonalook watched Sundu devour the leg, then held up his two fingers again. He bounced his hand like the rabbit as he had before, and smacked it into his other hand.

"Bah!" said Noonalook and laid his hand over.

Sundu and Noonalook laughed again, but Sundu's eyes flashed up behind Noonalook, and he screamed. Noonalook turned to see a group of men standing behind him. He reached for his knife, but a club came down on his head, knocking him unconscious.

Noonalook woke with a pounding headache and nausea. All was dark except for the orange and gray coals, which had once been their fire. He couldn't see out of one eye and found it caked shut with dried blood. He slowly sat up, holding his aching head, trying to remember what had happened.

He rubbed the dried blood away from his eye and looked around. He was alone. Where was the boy? He remembered Sundu screaming, then he remembered the men. And they were men, like himself, not like the strange looking ones before. The men had taken Sundu.

"Sundu!" Noonalook called out, but there was no response.

Noonalook stood, and dizziness overcame him. He caught himself on the lean-to, but his weight was too much for the structure, and it collapsed with him. He rolled over and got to his hands and knees.

"Sundu!" he called out much louder, but there was still no response.

How long had he been lying on the ground? How far could they have gotten? If Sundu had heard him, and if he was able, he would have answered back. If they were too far away, he could have trouble finding them.

He reached for his knife and found it missing. He needed it to get the boy back again. He crawled around the campsite, searching the ground, but couldn't find it.

The rabbit was gone, too, as well as the curing fur, and the flint rocks. Those men had taken everything.

He sat down to determine what to do next, but the pain in his head prevented him from thinking clearly. He knew he needed to track down those people that had taken Sundu, and he needed a weapon. He didn't have time to make another knife or spear, and he didn't have the materials. He crawled back to the fallen lean-to and dug out a stick he could use as a club. It was about four feet long, thick and heavy, and better than nothing. He used it to stand and steady himself. He walked around the camp, looking at the ground for tracks, trying to find the direction the men had gone. It was difficult to see in the dark, and his eyes were still blurry from the headache, but he did find their trail.

He looked off in the darkness where the trail led, hoping to see firelight or some clue as to where the men had taken Sundu, but he saw nothing.

He followed the trail through dawn, still not finding the men or even where they had slept for the night. He guessed they had walked all night, which meant they hadn't traveled far from their home.

Noonalook was angry at himself for building a fire big enough to be seen across the land. He knew better and blamed himself for assuming no one else was around. Noonalook had been deceived by the beauty and serenity of the mountains and had unknowingly let his guard down. It was a costly mistake that he was now paying for.

The trail led toward the mountains, and he followed it for hours, up and down the hills and valleys, through the long grasses and tree groves. He was hungry and thirsty, but thoughts of Sundu scared or in pain raced through his mind. He had lost everything for Sundu, and now he had lost Sundu.

Noonalook understood Sundu would be better off living with a tribe than he would an old man. Still, Noonalook didn't know anything about the men that had taken the boy. If he knew those people were kind and would take care of Sundu, then he would abandon his search and head south, but those men had met him with violence, and he feared what they might do to Sundu. Noonalook didn't know why they hadn't killed him when he had been unconscious, but when he caught up to them, he would make them wish they had.

He came to a stream where he knelt and drank. He sat at the edge to rest when he noticed there was no trail on the other side. Where he sat, the footprints disappeared into the water, but there were none on the opposite side leading away. They had used the stream to cover their trail. Noonalook knew what they had done because he had done it himself. Once in the water, they had either walked upstream or downstream, then simply stepped out someplace else. He needed to find where they had exited.

He crossed the stream and looked for any clues as to which direction they could have gone. The water was stinging cold, so Noonalook couldn't imagine anyone walking in it for very long. He looked upstream then downstream. He searched for anything suspicious but found nothing out of the ordinary. He had hoped to see people or caves or smoke or some such in the distance indicating which way they might have gone.

Noonalook took a stone from the stream. It was heavy and about half the size of his head, and placed it in the grass near the bank. Should he go in the wrong direction, he would look for the stone and know where he'd started from. Walking downstream in the water would have been easier than walking upstream, so he walked along the edge of the water, following the current, and looked for traces of the men's tracks.

He walked along the bank until midday and decided the men had not walked downstream. As he walked back upstream, he couldn't help but wonder if he had been following the correct trail at all. Last night had been a blur, and it had been so dark, so what if he'd stumbled upon someone else's path again? What if he never found the way they'd taken? Would this mean he should give up? How long would he wander about searching for Sundu before he would freeze to death?

He eventually passed his marker stone, scrutinizing the ground along the stream for close to half an hour, searching for tracks. Ahead, a footprint in the mud caught his eye, and his heart jumped. He hurried to it and found a fresh footprint leading out of the water. He searched along the bank and found more prints, and one of them was a child's. It had to be Sundu's footprint.

He walked away from the stream, feeling elated, and followed their path through the grass. He was confident that he was on the right trail. He followed it for close to ten minutes until he came to a dead end. He searched the vicinity, not finding a trace of tracks or trail. The men were still trying to hide their way and had doubled back.

Noonalook returned to the water and looked for more footprints as he worked his way upstream. Farther down, he found prints along the edge, going into and out of the water. He walked northeast with the setting sun at his back and his shadow before him growing longer.

Close to dark, the path turned from the stream and headed north, taking Noonalook up a hill. The smells of smoke and cooking meat wafted at the peak, but Noonalook couldn't tell from where they came. The wind had a funny way of moving odors around, but he knew he had to be close to the source of the smells, though visually, there was nothing.

He followed the trail down the hill and through the valley. He shivered as the chilly wind whipped through the valley, still carrying the smells of fire and food. The path disappeared at the foot of a steep, rocky hill. The stones and boulders made it difficult and dangerous to climb. He was out of breath, and his muscles ached as he finally reached the top where he sat to rest and look around. The mountains before him were enormous, and blocked half of the starry night sky.

Behind him, his old home, blocked by the

hills he had climbed, was gone forever. He would never find it again, nor would he be able to find the cave he and Sundu had stayed in. His old life was gone, and the new life he faced now was full of uncertainty, and if he couldn't find Sundu, loneliness. Maybe traveling this far away was bringing him closer to his wife and son in the other life. He remembered gazing at the mountains from his home, always curious what they looked like up close. He never thought he would ever be here.

Something caught the corner of Noonalook's eye, but when he looked, nothing was there. He patiently watched the area then glimpsed a light through the trees below as the breeze blew the leaves around. It was firelight, and that's where Sundu had to be. He crept down the side of the rocky hill, trying to be as quiet as possible.

About halfway down, Noonalook stepped on a loose stone. It rolled out from under him, and he fell, tumbling and sliding down the hill, bringing with him a lot of other loose rocks and debris. He landed on the ground in a pile of rubble.

Loud voices erupted from the camp after hearing Noonalook's fall. Noonalook quickly stood and looked for his club, but he had lost it somewhere on his way down. There was no time to retrieve it or look for another and ran to hide.

A few sparse bushes to hide behind was all he could find. He crouched behind them as the voices drew closer. Several men ran into the area with spears and knives ready, investigating the sound they had heard. When they came to the pile of rocks Noonalook had brought down, they inspected them, then looked up at the hill and back down to the stones. They turned and squinted into the darkness. Noonalook sensed they knew a man had fallen down the hill and not some clumsy animal. The men whispered together in an unfamiliar language. One of the men spoke to the others while pointing about their surroundings, then they separated and searched the area.

Noonalook knew it wouldn't be long before he was found. One of the men with a spear passed near Noonalook, then stopped and turned around. Noonalook's heart raced, and his blood pounded in his ears as he watched the man stare at the bush he hid behind. The man took a few steps toward the Noonalook, pushing his spear out before him. Could the man see him? Noonalook had two choices, run or fight, but he didn't have a chance to decide. The man stepped around the bush and spotted Noonalook. Just as the man opened his mouth to yell a warning, Noonalook pulled on the spear, bringing the man closer to Noonalook. Noonalook punched the man in the throat, then kicked him in the groin. The man doubled over, gagging, and fell. Noonalook grabbed the spear and ran. The man finally cried out in a raspy voice, and all eyes turned to Noonalook. Shouting, the men converged on Noonalook, but he kept running.

A camp had been set up in front of a massive cave entrance. The few women cooking at the bonfire, and the old men warming themselves around it, stopped and stared as he approached. Noonalook looked for Sundu, but didn't see him or any other children, and assumed they were in the cave. He tossed the spear aside as he ran toward the cavern.

"Sundu!" Noonalook shouted.

He had almost made it to the camp when someone jumped on his back.

"Sun-!" he tried to yell again, but his face slammed into the ground, cutting off his words and air. Hands were on him, pulling, pushing, squeezing, hitting, and scratching. He fought to raise his head up just enough to get a gasp of air to call again.

"Sundu!" he cried out as loud as he could. "Sun-!" and again, his face was pushed into the earth. He had to know if the boy was here. He had to know Sundu was safe before he died. The angry voices around him began to fade, and bright light seemed to shine in his eyes, though they were closed. His body convulsed as his lung starved for oxygen. He inhaled dirt and choked, then a familiar word cut through the chaos.

"Hendi!"

The hands on his body stopped.

"Hendi!" came the voice again.

Someone let go of Noonalook's head, and he looked up, coughing and wheezing. Sundu stood before him, holding his new knife and pointing it at the men who held Noonalook. He was clean and wore new, warm skins. A young woman approached and stopped behind Sundu, watching in disbelief.

"Noonalook!" cried a girl's voice.

To his right, two young girls ran to Noonalook crying, leaving two more girls tied to a tree.

"Dundo, Noonalook!" said one of the girls as they lay on the ground in front of him. Their hands were tied, and their faces were dirty from dirt sticking to their tears.

Noonalook recognized the girls as the ones

taken from his village. They had once been part of the kids who had ridiculed him. They had hated him then but were now glad to see him. Their pleading eyes told Noonalook they wanted to go home.

Two men grabbed the girls and dragged them back to the girls tied to the tree. Another man stepped from behind Noonalook to get a better look at the old man. He knelt before Noonalook and studied his face. Noonalook remembered the man as the chief of the tribe that had invaded his village. After a moment, he looked back at Sundu and the woman.

"Tu gaunan, lo, Sundu?" asked the chief.

"Noonalook, Samisane," said Sundu. "Garlona."

When the chief looked back at Noonalook, there was something in the chief's eyes, like a smile. This man reminded Noonalook of himself when he had been younger and healthier. The chief stood and stepped back.

The camp turned still and quiet, with only the crackling of the fire. Sundu walked closer to the men with the little knife still pointed at them.

"Akinik, Noonalook," said Sundu.

The men looked at each other, then up to the chief. When their leader nodded, the men released Noonalook and backed away. Before Noonalook could get up, Sundu ran to him and fell to his knees. Sobbing, he dropped the knife and hugged Noonalook tightly. Noonalook stretched out his arm and brought it around Sundu, returning the hug and patting him on the back. As the woman knelt beside Sundu, putting her arm around him, Noonalook looked at her, then around at the others.

"Clenemo, sondul dee," Sundu said to the woman.

The woman never looked at Sundu but kept her eyes on Noonalook. The woman was young, in her early twenties, with long, dark wavy hair. The eyes that watched Noonalook were reddish-brown, like the bark of a pine tree.

"Noonalook," said Sundu, then he put a hand on the woman. "Dendaya."

Noonalook had heard that word before. He knew the word. The boy had spoken it many times when they had first started their journey. Mother. It took a moment for Noonalook to comprehend what had happened. He had been so frightened and determined to find Sundu that he hadn't put all the pieces together. He looked back at the four girls from his tribe and the other people around him, then back to Sundu and his mother. Had he really found Sundu's tribe? Or, rather, it seemed Sundu's tribe had found him. He didn't understand how it had happened, and it didn't seem possible. His head whirled with all that had happened and felt as if he were dreaming, but he wasn't.

"Noonalook?" Sundu asked, looking concerned.

Noonalook smiled and patted the boy on the head, then he laughed, and Sundu laughed with him.

"Noonalook," said the woman.

Noonalook nodded.

"Thera," she said, placing her hand to her chest.

"Thera," Noonalook repeated.

"Lo, mobuma, lo nellono garlona," Sundu said to his mother in a serious tone, and Noonalook stopped laughing.

Thera's eyes moved from Sundu to Noonalook, examining him from head to foot. She raised her hand and traced gentle fingers down the scars on Noonalook's face, arms, and chest. His smile disappeared. No one had ever touched his old injuries like that before, and he didn't like the feeling it gave him. He quickly stood and looked around. He'd returned Sundu to his mother and tribe as he had set out to do, and now it was all over. If the men would let him leave, then he would be on his way, beginning his long journey south.

He patted Sundu on the head.

"Sundu, mawpumo. Dunto," Noonalook said with a smile.

Everyone watched him turn and walk away from the camp. Now he would start his new life, and he would do it alone.

"Hendi!" he heard behind him, but it wasn't Sundu.

He turned to find Thera following him. She and Sundu each took Noonalook's hands to pull him gently back to the camp, leading him to the fire and sat him down. Before him, the flames caressed the carcass of a deer cooking over it.

Thera took a piece of the meat and gave it to Noonalook. He smiled and nodded to her as he gladly took it. Others came and tore off pieces for themselves and their children, who had hidden in the cave.

People talked as they ate, and the camp returned to normal. Noonalook sat between Sundu and Thera as he ate. A smiling elderly lady put a thick, warm fur over Noonalook's shoulders, covering his back. A minute later, another woman brought him a bladder of water with a smile. He nodded and smiled back. He took another bite, and someone offered his old flint knife to him. The chief held the knife, blade in hand, and the handle facing Noonalook. Noonalook slowly took the knife. The chief nodded to Noonalook with a look of sternness, then grinned, and turned to join the rest of the men in eating and talking.

Noonalook was confused at their generosity. What had Sundu told his tribe about him? Perhaps it was because he had rescued the boy and brought him back home. These people were not like his own. Back there, he had been a great man, but they didn't treat him that way. Here, he was nothing, but they treated him as a great man.

After eating and drinking, the warmth of the fire, and warm fur on his back, Noonalook began to feel sleepy. He needed to find a place to sleep so he could be on his way early in the morning. He put the knife back in his belt and slowly and painfully stood. He drew little attention until he returned the fur and water bladder to the women who had given them to him, and he walked out of the camp again.

"Noonalook!" Sundu cried out.

Noonalook turned around to Sundu, running toward him.

"Hendi, Noonalook!" said the boy.

Sundu grabbed Noonalook's hand and tried to pull him back to camp, but Noonalook didn't budge. Noonalook pointed up, over the hills, back to his old home.

"Junda," said Noonalook, even though he knew he would never find it again.

"Hendi!" Sundu grabbed Noonalook around the waist, holding tightly and bawling. "Garlona!" Sundu said through sobs.

Noonalook didn't know what to do. He had to leave the boy eventually, and sooner would be better. Noonalook had grown attached to Sundu, and he didn't want to make it worse.

Thera walked toward him with a smile. She took Noonalook's hand and brought it to her face, gently rubbing the back of his hand against her cheek. She kissed his hand as her dark eyes gazed up at him. Noonalook was unsure of what to say, think, or do.

"Garlona," Sundu said again, looking up at him.

When he heard it again, Noonalook realized Sundu had spoken that word before, but he couldn't remember the meaning of it. His mind was a mess of confusion. Thera pulled Noonalook's hand, and Sundu pulled the other, and together, they led him back to camp. Noonalook wasn't sure what they wanted, but he let himself be taken. Everyone watched as Noonalook was led up into the cave.

Inside the cave was another smaller fire giving little warmth and light. Furs laid about in different areas of the cave with people lying on them. Thera and Sundu led Noonalook through the maze of sleeping people to a place near the cave wall where there were hides spread out.

Sundu lay down on one of the fur mats, covered himself with one, and patted the bedding next to him for Noonalook. Noonalook smiled briefly and unsure. He looked at Thera, who nodded and smiled. She pulled Noonalook's knife from his belt and placed it on the ground against the wall. She knelt and offered a place for Noonalook between Sundu and herself. Noonalook hesitantly lay down and looked from Sundu to Thera. Thera lay down close to him and covered him and herself. She scooted to him and wrapped her arm around him, holding him tightly to her. The warmth of her body as she pressed against him brought sensations of comfort and pleasure to Noonalook he never thought he would feel again. In the faint, flickering light, Sundu smiled at him.

"Garlona," Sundu said quietly once more, then closed his eyes.

That word again. Noonalook still couldn't remember what it meant, but with a little time, he would learn it. Noonalook put his hand over Thera's and squeezed it softly, then wiped his eyes. He found tears but didn't know why because he was very far from sad. He kissed Thera's hand and closed his eyes and slept.

At one time, Noonalook had been an insignificant man and accomplished nothing, but not anymore. At one time Noonalook had lost favor with his tribe, and had no wife and son, but not anymore. Those sad days were over, and things would be better from now on.

# ABOUT THE AUTHOR

T Reeves lives in Oklahoma. He received his BFA from the University of Oklahoma, where he studied film and animation. He has written several screenplays and won a few awards with his fiction. He is married and has two kids, one cat, two ducks, and several chickens.

Made in the USA
Monee, IL
17 October 2020

45058342R00094